[The Pigeon

A novel by

[MOTAZ H MATAR]

Copyright Registration Service
Ref: 2070107

DEDICATION

To my wife, Liz Matar.
For the wonderful journey, and for many years to
come.

ACKNOWLEDGEMENTS

Being in this world is finding oneself on a continued quest to belong. This journey is characterised by misunderstandings, separation and conflict. My hope is that this story will help bridge the gap between two different worlds: the East and the West, and to allow us to understand each other better, or at least attempt to.

First of all, I would like to thank God, my creator, for giving me the ability to dream, to dare to be creative, and for opening the door of spirituality for me. Next comes my parents and my family without whom I wouldn't be where I am today. I also want to take the opportunity to sincerely thank my teacher, Dr. Prof. Joachim Friedmann, who has been a great mentor and has supported me in shaping the story. Last but not least, I am thankful to my friends and supporters who believe in me: without them I wouldn't even be a writer today. I have no words to express how I am feeling. Please accept my heartfelt thanks

FOREWORD

After the war broke out in their home country, many Syrians migrated to Europe in an attempt to find a new place to settle.

This is the story of belonging. This is the story of finding somewhere to call home.

On attempting to write this book, I realised that this story was an intrinsic part of my self and it became important to tell it accurately. I didn't have to do much soul searching: the story of the pigeon whisperer was already inhabiting me. My mother is Syrian and I have personally experienced the great escape to the West myself.

Whether you seek to find your home in faith, in love, in art, or in your DNA, I hope that this book becomes a tool of introspection or a map for your physical journey of finding your home, your destination, where you are meant to be.

PRELUDE

Evil is infectious, like a disease. Goodness is not.

I opened my window and it was chaos. The world had been bombed and shelled and everything was scattered to pieces. The snipers who hid behind glass windows were playing games, shooting down birds and humans alike. They would make bets on how fast and how many birds they could shoot down. The sky no longer belonged to the birds. Syria was no longer my home.

Belonging to the world was hard, finding somewhere to call home even harder. "Think again," I said to myself. "Think before you leave. Think before you make decisions that you might regret. Think about saving your life, even if it means being away from those you love, even if it means saying goodbye to beautiful feather-like creatures which had stolen my heart. Think again. For how long can your soul endure the suffering caused by rifles, snipers, jet fighters and political tyranny? Pack your bags and leave this place. Leave the war."

Maybe I would find another place to call home. Maybe I could learn to live again, even in the cold winter of Europe, welcomed as a refugee.

The night fell and the gunshots eased. Yasser was waiting outside my door in an old beat-up car. He honked the horn. It was a special one, one that you would not miss at night, looking from the window of your room into the world.

I walked down. We drove off. Something startled Yasser: a handmade basket that I was carrying with me. He gave me a look of alarm. In the basket were five pigeons, my finest and most precious ones. They were rare, but they were also lucky, because they had somehow survived the war.

We were on our way to somewhere. To nowhere. To the unknown. To hell. Yasser never told me where we were going; I just rode along the dusty road. I trusted him, I had to. We were heading towards our destiny. To die, or to become prisoners of fate and war. We sat in the car for hours and waited for the sun to rise one more time; probably for the last time. Yasser smoked a whole pack of cigarettes; I thought he would die from the smoke inhalation before sunrise; he was inhaling and exhaling so deeply. The car smelled like ash and butts. We were suffocating. I was doubly suffocating. Suffocating from the inside of my soul. I wanted a way out of this mess. I wanted out from it all.

"Will you stop smoking?! You are going to kill yourself!"

Yasser looked at me and blew the smoke in my face. I coughed, hardly breathing.

A knock on the window alarmed us. It was slow and creepy. Yasser rolled down his window, and a man sneaked his head in. His face was covered with a red and white scarf. He looked Jordanian. The scarf covered his features. Yasser pulled a brown envelope from his jacket. The man gestured to Yasser to wait. Yasser rolled up his window and we waited in anticipation.

"It's happening!"

The man walked back to his car, then turned and started heading back to us. Yasser rolled down his window.

"OK, come!" said the man with the red and white scarf to Yasser.

"What about the car, do we leave it here?" I asked Yasser.

Yasser stepped out of the car without saying anything. He took his bags from the trunk. I followed him in hesitation.

"Are you going to leave the car here?" I asked him.

"I'm selling my dad's car!" he told me as he closed the trunk and walked to a green van parked in front of us. The van drove us to a bus stop which was a couple of miles ahead. Yasser was selling his dad's car so we could leave. Yasser had never told any of his family members where he was going. He just left.

We said goodbye to the red-scarfed man as he handed us our fake passports. He departed with a cold goodbye. His final words resonated in my ears.

"You are on your own now. In this life you are always alone. Remember that!" He disappeared, hopping into his van and drove away.

***

"You can't take your birds with you!" the driver said to me, when we arrived at the border, but I insisted. Yasser pulled me aside and scolded me. He reprimanded me like I was a little boy. We were so close to freedom. I was going to ruin everything. It was a moment I will remember forever.

"There is no way I'm going back!" Yasser said to me as the bus headed towards the Turkish border.

An army officer came to check our IDs, passenger by passenger. My heart raced. When he saw me, he stopped and gazed at the empty basket sitting on my lap.

"Don't fucking say a word." Yasser angrily whispered in my ear. The engine was ignited and I heard the sounds of the birds flying high and flapping their wings. I could see them from the window, hovering over us like paper-kites saying their goodbyes. My eyes began to fill with water as I gazed at the display of the moving scenery as if it was from a movie, fading out into the next scene.

I am the lost one. I bang my head against the thick walls to find my home, to find my place, to find where I belong. I remain still, standing in the centre. I look up and find myself surrounded by all the people I know. Some of them I don't know and each one of them is pulling me in their own direction. But I resist and I insist. I am the bull. I resist and continue to resist, determined to belong and find home one day.

1
THE BULL

I have always wondered why my family has named me Dabbour, the wasp. I have always felt insignificant, just like a fly. I said goodbye to Syria, my home. I wonder if we, as refugees, will be asked about our sins and the suffering we endured? Our ear drums tortured, almost pierced, by bomb shells and fighter engines. It was the fifth year and counting of the war, the never-ending war, when I breathed the air of European life for the first time.

On the train to Germany, I felt that home was not far away, that I could finally be somewhere and live. Life had just began in Germany. A different life than the one I had known before.

Those who are afraid to live will never have a life and will never be able to live, I thought. There was no point in being scared. Losing and winning is all part of the game of life. Sometimes you lose, a few times you win, but the very ideal of losing and winning changes over time. It no longer defines us. It defies us, destroys us, or shapes us into who we are; we become a living combination of our losses and our victories.

After a few months of landing in this foreign land, we were able to learn a few words. We could order coffee and food, ask about the time, understand the curse words, and we found ourselves slowly blending into the German culture. To the Germans we were outsiders and most of them didn't want to get to know us, except for a few who were aware of our story and empathised with us. Their looks translated into stares of suspicion, fear, and confusion. We felt that the Germans were not happy with us being let into their country. Some refugees became rebellious, breaking the rules, even irritating the rest of us. I once saw a guy speaking Arabic loudly in the train, without any concern for others. I saw another breaking the rules. I witnessed all this and felt helpless, very often hopeless. The Germans were no angels either. I purposely chose to remain silent to a lot of things I saw.

We lived in Berlin. I loved Berlin. And sometimes I hated Berlin. The smell of freshly baked bread, the vintage green walls of the underground stations and their black and white WWII pictures on display as if stuck in time and oblivious to the war raging through my own war-ravaged country. Sometimes the smell of bread would mix with the smell of weed and fresh air. Some other times, it would blend with stinky urine. A strange combination of love and hate. Of modernity and of the mundane, of privilege taken for granted.

The train approached, brakes screeching on the metal. It was not our train yet; our train was a few minutes late and Yasser stood there, restless, close to the edge of the platform. Yasser teased me about being a nerd and wanting to learn the language and harassed me about my crush for my German language teacher, Zara, whom he could see I liked.

"I know why you go to the German classes," he said to me. "I saw the way you were looking at her curves!"

I knew Zara was out of my reach. I called her Zahra, a flower. Had I met her in a different time and place, things could have been different. We were so different; our paths were worlds apart. Everything was different. Sometimes the difference can hide something, something that the bare eye cannot comprehend and that only time can unveil.

My heart skipped another beat when I remembered her and another beat out of fear, not love, this time, but from what was unfolding in front of us. Two police officers appeared in front of me and I stood still, motionless. It was a tall German man, and a female officer was by his side.

"Can I see your IDs?" she asked us.

I searched my pocket and my jeans, but I couldn't find my wallet. I must have left it at the refugee home. If at least one of us had an ID, we could have avoided a lot of the trouble that was about to happen. I looked at Yasser, and he told the police officer that we had left our IDs at the refugee accommodation. But I could see that Yasser was already thinking of a plan: he was thinking of running away. The two officers were communicating in German. Yasser came closer to me and quickly whispered in my right ear.

"When I run, you run, don't look back!" he said to me.

I was hoping they would not hear him, but they could clearly feel suspicion. Yasser was taking advantage of the two distracted officers mumbling on their swooshing walkie-talkies. It was at this moment that something caught my attention and my heart began racing.

The train approached. People gathered near the platform. Yasser was getting ready to run. It was the perfect moment to blend in with the crowds of people. The police officers were on alert; their walkie-talkies swooshed even more. On hearing the next train announcement, Yasser decided to make his move. I started running. As fast as I could. Police swiftly started chasing us. Yasser ran towards the stairs, I ran in an opposite direction. The stomping noise of my feet hitting the ground caught the attention of people around. I was not running away from the police. I jumped onto the tracks to save an injured pigeon that was lying directly on the far rail. I grabbed him and was desperately trying to get us back safely onto the platform. But I was clearly struggling to do so, as I was holding the pigeon in my hand.

Something strange and divine happened: a hand was stretched out of nowhere to save me. Amongst the utter chaos, it felt like it was God's hand reaching out to me. Everything happened so fast. The train driver cursed and shouted, brakes continued to screech on the metal but whose hand was it? I looked up, my body still lying on the ground of the platform, arrested by police and a pigeon squeezed in my hand so tightly that I thought she would die from suffocation. I refused to let go as if I was holding on to the last hope of finding home again. I only saw feet then hands. Then feet again. I saw the feet of the man who saved me. I was hurried and pushed and shackled by the police. I was able to get a glance of the man who saved me — only briefly — the man with the godly hand. All attention was directed towards me, all eyes were locked on me. Everyone stood there at the station like they were watching a movie. People wondered what would happen to me after my arrest. I wanted to scream and shout and tell them that the movie is over. I desperately wanted to tell them to leave. To leave now. The show was over.

***

Ashamed, I sat facing Anna in the interrogation room, neon lights flickering, hands on the table. The wind was blowing outside; it was cold. Her gun was hanging on her side. Her police uniform was so nice, projecting prestige, made of high-quality material; German quality. Another police officer stood outside; I could see his shadow behind the door. Suddenly, Anna hit the table hard and I thought it was going to break. Her hand must have hurt really bad.

"Are you okay?" I asked Anna, looking at her hand, which was turning red.

It was awkward. She was the one who was supposed to start interrogating me, not the other way round. She dismissed my question and the interrogation began. It didn't feel like an interrogation, although I knew I was in big trouble. I felt safe. I felt justice. Strange! I was aware that I had done something wrong, several wrongs in fact, but I felt comfortable, until Anna told me I could be deported because I had broken several German laws. That's when I sensed my own fear. I needed to defend myself. I felt the urge to say something.

"I was only trying to save the injured pigeon," I said.

"You jumped on the train tracks. You ran away from the police." she said. "Verschtest du?"

I nodded. I had to acknowledge that I had understood what she said. Where I come from, everything is different. The rules are more lenient. People break them with so much ease. If you do something wrong, you will find that there are so many ways that you can get away with it. For example, telling the police officer that you are their relative or asking them about someone they know or buying them a pack of cigarettes or greasing someone's palm to make them feel like they're the real deal. Sometimes if the offending is quite serious, you can bribe the police officer from under the table. The only rule: just make sure nobody finds out. But here in Germany, it was different. The law was the law and I was a refugee. I had to abide.

Anna left the room, slamming the door behind her. A few minutes passed, and I could hear her talking to the police officer standing outside. I was able to overhear a few words: "trouble," "the other guy," and "deportation." That's all.

Could they have been talking about Yasser?, I thought. Maybe. Or was it about me?

Anna came back in and walked towards me. She stared at me from head to toe. I waited for her to speak.

"I'm going to send you back home."

"Which home? I don't have a home!" I said.

The words fell heavy on her ears like a bang.

"To where you came from," she said.

"I can't go back to a war zone! I will die. My birds are already dead!"

"Bird? You think this is a joke? Listen kid, if you want to stay in Germany, you have to learn to follow the rules," said Anna. She was fierce. Tough. I wondered why she was calling me a kid and why she even considered me as one. Did I look that innocent? Naïve? Stupid?

"Don't deport me!" I said to Anna. I almost begged, aware that I had to maintain some level of dignity.

Anna left the room again. This time, the conversation with the other police officer was more tense. They were both angry at each other. I could hear them better this time.

"Are you aware that you will have to accept full responsibility for this?" the other police officer asked Anna.

"Don't you tell me how to do my job, okay?" said Anna.

She stormed back into the interrogation room and walked towards me. She didn't stop until she was close to me. I could feel her warm breath in my ears. Just when I thought she would not come any closer, she did.

"This is your last chance. You can go home now. I don't want to see you here again."

I was confused. Home? What did she mean? The other police officer opened the door. He pulled me up from the chair and shoved me towards the door. There was a long hall. We walked. I felt relieved. I was happy to be heading towards the door, any door. Doors could be paths towards freedom and salvation; sometimes they could be paths to endings. Sometimes, they could lead to new beginnings.

As we headed towards the exit, I remembered the injured pigeon and I froze in my steps. The officer's grip was still firm on my arm. I tried to move to set my arm free from his grip.

"What happened to the pigeon?" I asked the police officer.

"She's dead. We buried her!" he said.

"What? Why did you do that?"

The police officer ignored my question and swiped his card to unlock the door. I could see the street before me and I felt the cold breeze blowing on my face.

"I don't want to see you here again, ever!" he told me. He wasn't very nice. Anna, despite her harshness, had a certain warmth to her, I thought to myself.

I stood outside. The wind was blowing even more harshly. Words on repeat were rumbling in my head:

We buried her, we buried her. My thoughts were racing. That couldn't be true, I thought to myself. I looked around. Everywhere. I searched for the pigeon thinking, hoping she was still alive. Hoping that should would still be breathing. I wanted to find her. Like a lover with a broken heart longing for love again, I started looking for the bird. I searched under the trees and in the garbage containers.

Then a voice came from behind calling. I stopped and turned to see where the voice was coming from.

"I know what you're looking for!" the voice said.

I swear I had seen this face before. I couldn't remember where.

"You were at the train station. You saved me!" I said. "But why are you following me? Are you stalking me?" I said. I was still angry.

I continued to search for the lost pigeon, purposely ignoring the man

"You are looking for the dead pigeon," he said.

"How do you know?" I said.

"I followed you to the police station," he said.

"So, you are a stalker! Leave me alone please!" I said.

I started to feel frustrated, like something was wrong. Why was that man following me? What did he want from me? I told him to leave me alone but he wouldn't. I insisted.

"Please go!" I said again.

"I know where you can find her," he said.

"You don't!"

"Sometimes you just need to accept the fact that something is lost and gone forever!" he said.

"You're lying! You don't know where she is!"

"Are you sure? Okay, come with me," said the man. "But I'm warning you: you're not going to be happy."

The man walked towards a tree and started digging up the mud with his bare hands.

"I saw them bury her here. Come look!" he said.

I didn't want to see her dead. I froze and stood still. At that point, I had to let go of any hope to find the pigeon alive. I had to face the reality that it had disappeared. There was no bird. It was gone. Dead.

***

We sat in a nearby cafe. It felt good to be in a warm place drinking coffee instead of being in prison or in a cold hall waiting to be sent back. This strange man and I were sitting face to face. We drank our coffee. We stared into the void. We didn't talk much. I was heart-broken. I was still hurt; all my attempts to save the bird had been in vain. I had risked my life for nothing. The man was speaking to me in an attempt to lighten the mood and the atmosphere filling this side of the otherwise empty café.

"Do you like your coffee,?" he asked me.

"It's good" I said. I still didn't feel like talking.

"I was there and saw what happened at the train station. Why did you do it?" he asked.

"I was trying to save her! She needed help." I said. I knew he didn't believe me.

"Why would anyone risk his own life to save an injured bird? You could have died, you know that?" the old man said.

Then he looked at me and noticed that I was not happy with what he said.

"I'm sorry. I didn't mean to say it that way!" said the man. "What's your name?"

"I am Dabbour," I said. "And you?"

"I'm Mr. Saleh."

Mr. Saleh was Syrian. He had been living in Germany for more than twenty years, I later learnt.

When he heard me speaking Arabic to Yasser, he knew straightaway where I came from. Did he happen to be there, by chance, to save my life, like an angel sent at the right time and landing at the right place?

"I'm sorry, did I say thank you to you? I asked. "Thank me for what? You don't have to. I happened to be there. I didn't really think. I just did what I had

19

to do," Mr. Saleh said. "What did they tell you at the police station?"

"They warned me that I could be deported if I did anything similar again." I said.

"That's it?" he asked. "Strange!" said Mr. Saleh.

"What do you mean by 'strange'?" I asked.

"They are usually stricter. To let you go like this? Hmmm…"

"What are you trying to tell me?" I asked.

"I'm saying that you need to be careful. You have to follow the rules if you want to succeed here," said Mr. Saleh. "I've been here for more than twenty years and I've never been in trouble once. I've seen how people get deported, especially refugees, do you understand?"

We were from two different generations. We thought differently. Mr. Saleh was wiser and more experienced. I was still fragile. I knew nothing. But there was a huge gap between the two generations. Mr. Saleh's generation had a much easier life. Our life was much harder – it was getting worse by the minute.

"When I was twenty years old, I wanted to leave Syria. After the war in 1967, I was fed up with the situation. I went to my dad and told him I wanted to go and study in Germany. It was so easy. I took a bus to Turkey and made my way to Germany. I didn't have an acceptance letter; I didn't know the language or anything. Nothing. I just landed in a new country. I found myself at the language centre. When I reached there that night, it was closed. I went to a bar that was close by and spent the night there until the next day. That was it. My journey had started."

"Really?" I asked. I could not believe how easy could have been for Mr. Saleh's generation. "Don't give them an excuse to deport you. That's my advice to you," he said.

I thanked him again for such precious advice. He must know how hard it is to be a refugee. For we all carry the heavy burden of those who came before us and who were unjustly accused of invading new territories and stealing other peoples' lands. Every refugee, whether good or bad, was an inherent part of the problem. Every single one of us was the problem. We were the problem.

"Don't let a few rotten apples ruin your success. I've seen a lot of people take the wrong path. You're a good apple, Dabbour, I think. Don't let it go wrong!" said Mr. Saleh.

I allowed my brain to process what Mr. Saleh had said. Then, my phone rang. It was Yasser. He was nearby, close to the café. I told him where we were. A few minutes passed and Yasser stormed in. Yasser's first reaction was not a happy one. He was not happy

that I had made a friend. Yasser couldn't help but notice Mr. Saleh's Kashmir jacket which gave him the ap-
pearance of a well-off senior citizen who owns a business. Elegantly dressed. Not ragged like us. Yasser was
charming but cunning. Both of them were completely
opposite in their attire, their attitude and in the way
they spoke to each other. They were so different in
everything.

"Hello, good to see you," said Mr. Saleh, but he
didn't mean it. I knew it. There was something off.

Yasser ordered himself a coffee and hurried for me
to leave. I asked him if we could stay another ten
minutes but Yasser was in a hurry. I excused myself to
leave.

"Okay, Mr. Saleh. It was a pleasure to meet you,
but we have to go."

"You too, Dabbour. Remember what I told you.
Do not get in trouble." said Mr. Saleh.

Yasser was not happy with what Mr. Saleh was saying. He couldn't help himself. He had to say something.

"Why do you let him talk to you like that?" Yasser
whispered in my ear. Mr. Saleh overheard him but my
friend couldn't care less. They both caught each other
staring in dislike and doubt. There was tension between the two. I didn't know what to do. Yasser felt
the need to confront Mr. Saleh with the same words.

"What kind of trouble?" asked Yasser.

"I'm giving him a piece of advice. You can use it too. It could be helpful to you too since you are both new here."

Mr. Saleh was nice and friendly, but Yasser took it upon himself to teach the old man a lesson — he felt offended and didn't like anyone to tell him what to do. Yasser would all of a sudden become hypersensitive and would take things personally just because he didn't want to listen. He was stubborn. His attitude benefited us sometimes, but not always.

"Hey, no one asked you for your advice!" said Yasser.

I took a deep breath. Mr. Saleh felt disrespected.

I didn't say a word. I didn't know what to do. I wanted to apologise or pull them away from each other. Mr. Saleh ignored Yasser's comment. This only made the situation worse and Yasser was boiling with anger. He felt provoked, big time.

"Aren't you going to say anything?" asked Yasser.

Mr. Saleh walked past Yasser, which made him feel like he was a mere shadow.

I rushed to the counter to try to pay for the coffee and then remembered I didn't have my wallet on me. Mr. Saleh pushed me aside.

"Your coffee is on me. Just go." said Mr. Saleh.

Yasser walked out of the cafe. The cashier called out to him. He hadn't paid for his drink.

"My dad will pay!" Yasser said pointing to Mr. Saleh and walked out. Mr. Saleh followed Yasser in frustration. I followed them.

"Hey, didn't you hear the cashier? You didn't pay for your coffee!" said Mr. Saleh to Yasser.

"Didn't you say it's on you?" Yasser asked sarcastically.

Mr. Saleh told Yasser that he had offered to pay for my coffee, not his.

"You can offer to buy it for me too; I'm your friend's friend." said Yasser.

"You have to pay for yours. I'm sorry!" said Mr. Saleh.

Mr. Saleh managed to absorb his frustration and anger. He thought for a second, then walked back inside and paid for the coffee. He came back outside, by which time Yasser was already leaving again. Yasser opened the door and wanted to go in. Mr. Saleh and Yasser both bumped shoulder to shoulder.

"I can pay for it, it's only two Euros." Yasser shouted.

Mr. Saleh walked away, not saying a word.

I saw Yasser pick up something from the ground and put it in his pocket. I didn't see what it was. By that time, Mr. Saleh was already gone.

"You were so mean to the man. He was nice!" I said.

"You are so naive!" said Yasser.

"What's wrong with you, Yasser? And will you stop smiling!?" I said.

Yasser pulled something from his back pocket and showed it to me. It was a wallet. It was Mr. Saleh's wallet.

"Oh my god, did you steal it?" I asked.

"I didn't steal anything. Your friend dropped it! Are you blind?" said Yasser.

"You need to give it back!" I said trying to snatch the wallet from Yasser but he was too fast. He put it back into his pocket.

"Don't even try. I will not give it back. Ever!"

If I had taken the wallet and ran away, I thought, Yasser would have followed me and knocked me down. He could even have kicked me out of the house. I would have to sleep outside by the staircase or in the street.

"Don't worry, he'll come back looking for it," Yasser said. We walked away.

***

Der, Die, Das. Dativ. Akkusativ. I couldn't focus. Yesterday's events kept playing on repeat in my mind.

I was thinking about the dead bird and being detained at the police station. I was light-struck every time she talked or waved or swayed her hair or explained a word. I was fixated on Zara, not the words written on the white board. Everything else was blurry. Except her words.

I waited for the students to leave. I wanted to talk to Zara and ask her something. I forgot what I wanted to say. She didn't even see me. She was busy attending to the exam papers and marking some student's paper. She was dedicated and serious about her job. I was also committed to studying but I struggled to manage. I was tired. I walked slowly towards her. I stuttered. I stood there and went blank. Zara already knew what I wanted and had also learnt her response very well. She reminded me what I wanted from her.

"I'm sorry. You can't redo the exam. No. I should expect you to start speaking to me in German now. You are level B1 now."

"I am trying..."

"Good, keep trying. I am busy now."

Zara ignored me and continued her work. I left the classroom and stood outside waiting for the elevator, ready to go home. I waited for a minute or two.

"You forgot to press the button," Zara said, smirking, as she pressed it for me. She was right behind me. It was as if her entire demeanour had changed as soon as she stepped out of the classroom. She was a woman now, not a teacher.

I felt too shy to be with her in the elevator. I couldn't bear her stunning beauty, so I decided to use the stairs instead. Zara saw me walking towards the stairs and she started laughing.

"Are you serious? There is no reason to be shy with me, right?" said Zara.

"Right!" I nodded.

In the tiny elevator, I saw her smiling at me in the reflection of the mirror. Zara noticed a tiny bruise on my face. It was from the fall last night and I tried to hide it with a scarf.

"What happened to you?" asked Zara.

"I fell." I said.

"Did you fall from your bike?" asked Zara.

"I fell on the train tracks!" I said.

"Train tracks?" asked Zara.

"I jumped to save an injured pigeon from getting hit by a train," I said.

Zara laughed. She just wouldn't believe it. She thought I was bluffing, lying. As we stepped outside, we didn't part ways. I told her there was no reason for me to lie. She told me she knew I was not a liar, but my story did not make sense to her. How could I prove to her what made sense and what didn't? How would I tell her about my life? About my hobby? There must have been a way to prove everything. If only she knew about my past. If only she knew about my hometown and the birds moving together like a mosaic in the sky. If only she knew what was my fault and what wasn't. If only she knew about those who get to choose their own home and those who simply couldn't.

The sun was about to set, and I asked Zara for a favour. I invited her to accompany me to a special place. She was hesitant. I promised that it was not going to take long. I wanted to show her the real sunset, something she probably had never seen before. Something she hadn't witnessed yet in Germany, her home country. She agreed. I took her by the hand and off we went. I was like a child running in the street. She allowed the child in me to shine and glow.

I took Zara to the Bellevue Bridge where the dapper pigeons lived. My favourite place in Berlin. This is where I felt most at home, and this place also helped me forget my first home. I hoped it would be our favourite place soon too. I felt so free, elated to be able to show Zara who I was and what I had been doing all my life. Maybe she would know me better — just a little. I was excited.

When we got there, the birds welcomed us by showing off: flying to a short height and then landing again.

"Beautiful!" Zara watched with anticipation.

"Are you ready?!" I asked excitedly.

Zara eyes glowed with the sunlight upon witnessing the amazing scene of the birds flying. Her curly blonde hair was undulating in the air. I grabbed a black plastic bag from my pocket and waved it in rhythm with her hair. I waved it again and the sound acted like a cue and the pigeons began to fly in the air. For the pigeons, this sound was similar to the sound of gunshots at the start of a race – and off they went. For me the sound of the gunshots reminded me of home.

The birds flew in circles around the orange sky and then slowed down upon their descent, landing right next to our feet. I waved the bag again and off they flew, this time higher, repeating their beautiful dance all over again in an organised pattern. Zara smiled. She asked me how I had done this trick. I felt melancholic. Zara could feel it. It was nostalgic, not that romantic anymore. The memories kicked in again.

"I was a pigeon breeder back home," I told Zara.

"What happened?" asked Zara.

"War. War happened!"

I dived into a state of recollection that I couldn't control. A tragic one. The red-coloured rooftop. I found myself feeling overwhelmed with emotions. I wiped my eyes with my sleeve. I tried to hide my tears so she couldn't see them. But of course she saw me crying, how could she not? I told her how I had lost the rest of the birds at the Turkish border. She could feel my pain. Her eyes watered. She almost wept with me.

I was completely overtaken by silence. I don't think she understood. Her watery eyes said it. Sometimes silence is better than any spoken word. I respected that. Silence in the presence of beauty is still beauty and oh how beautiful she was just standing there. I chose not to speak and allowed myself to indulge in her being and in her beauty. It felt good to just be there with her. I felt like a boy again; childish and naïve.

It got dark really quickly as our time together flew by. Why, I wondered? Zara took a step forward. I kneeled down to tie my shoelace. I looked up at her and smiled. Near my feet, I saw a pigeon. Zara knowingly walked two steps forward. I swiftly picked up the bird and hid her in my jacket. I stole her, you see. I stole the bird like Zara had stolen my heart.

We walked back, and both of us took a different train home. It was the beginning of a new chapter for me. It was the introduction of a new Dabbour.

***

Where I lived, I shared a small studio with Yasser in the refugee housing. It was a tiny room which was only big enough to accomodate the two of us. It was fitted with a window overlooking the street. Berlin was neat and clean, nothing like I have ever seen before. Quiet. Warm lights, which I liked. I loved everything about Berlin except the winter. I wasn't sure if it was mutual, the winter probably hated me and everything about me too.

The room was small. I slept on the top bed. It was a good way to avoid Yasser when I didn't feel like talking, pretending I was asleep. I was not a talker. Yasser was. I didn't mind it most of the time. I preferred silence.

"Are you asleep?" Yasser asked. I didn't say a word. I was in my own world and not in the mood for a chat.

"Come on, I know you're awake!" said Yasser.

"What do you want?" I said.

"It seems like you are still mad at me," said Yasser.

"No, I'm fine really. I'm just trying to sleep."

"Come on, it's just a wallet. Cheer up. We'll give it back."

Why didn't I believe Yasser? I had a feeling it was a mistake to travel with him as a companion. We were friends, but not that close. We were Syrians but very different. Maybe we were on that journey together because we come from the same country and had lived in the same neighbourhood. Like a childhood friend forced upon me by blood or proximity. Someone I had

never purposely chosen. He just happened to be there.
A part of my life. A part of my everything, everything
I took for granted. I went along. I never questioned. I
never thought how and why this had happened. I
thought I knew Yasser but I didn't. I barely knew myself. I was about to pay the price for not knowing anything, including myself.

That night was long. Really long. One of the long-
est nights in my life, and black, so black. There were a
few minutes, probably less than half an hour of silence.
The kind of silence that precedes the storm. A storm
that was lurking in the room. What I didn't know was
that Yasser wanted something from me. He said he
was going to introduce me to some guys. I told him
that it was late and I didn't feel like meeting anyone
new. He convinced me that it would not take long. He
always did the talking and did it so well. He was so
charming and convincing, luring and manipulating, so
much so that you eventually gave in and followed his
steps. Do you manipulate your best friend? Do you try
hard to lie to your best friend thinking he will believe
your lies? What was it about Yasser that made me suspicious? It wasn't anything he said, but I knew deep
inside that he was hiding something. Yasser took his
bike. I didn't have a bike so I rode behind him. He had
an extra seat. The Germans were so good at sleeping
at night. We were not. The feeling of being strangers

was intensified by our different culture and habits. They slept at night. We woke up at night like owls. They spoke less. We spoke more. They were quiet. We were loud. They hardly had any babies. We bred so many. Two different worlds were coming together. What are the odds?

Yasser parked his bike two blocks away from the underground station. I felt like I was hiding behind him like his shadow. I was scared. Terrified.

"Why are you walking behind me? Man up. We're not doing anything wrong." said Yasser.

This was Yasser's way of making himself believe that he was not doing anything wrong. We walked up to the train station. There was a guy standing there. He was about our age, wearing a hoodie, a black hoodie. The colour just blended in with the night so well. The guy was Ihsan. He had been to the German classes once or twice, but we never actually talked. One of the Syrians who had travelled to Germany with the flock of migrants over the past few years.

Yasser told me to keep my mouth shut and not say a word. We walked towards Ihsan and shook hands. Both him and Yasser looked at each other in a frozen stare and didn't blink. Yasser knew what to do. He walked away and I followed him.

We reached a dead end. There were bushes around us and Yasser was searching the bushes for something.

He became hyper. Nervous. He moved faster. Suddenly, he started going around in circles.

"What's going on?" I asked.

"We are doomed!" He said.

I didn't understand anything.

Yasser took out his phone. He had a knife tied to his waist under his belt. Why would he carry a knife? Yasser dialled a number on his phone and waited for the person on the other end to answer. I heard the phone ring.

"Who are you calling?" I asked.

I heard a man with a thick voice answer, his voice vibrating on the line. The sound was muffled and unrecognisable to me. Yasser talked faster, as if he was on fast forward mode. Hearts were beating and adrenaline was pumping. I could feel the rush of angry emotions running through his veins.

"Where the hell is the Blumen Kaufen?" asked Yasser.

Flowers? Was Yasser selling flowers? It was Yasser's code word for something. I knew it. He started screaming.

"Ihsan is going to kill you!" he said in Arabic. He lowered his voice when he said it. "He's going to kill you!"

I felt fear crawling into my blood. I knew I was stupid. I didn't know what was going on. Yasser hung up and walked back to where Ihsan was. I followed him, of course.

On the way I saw a bunch of stray pigeons hanging near the platform. I stopped. I pulled a seed pouch to feed one of them, and then the rest gathered around me. I was going to feed them the whole bag happily but something told me not to. Those seeds might be of use later. As I walked behind Yasser, he noticed the pigeons starting to follow us. He turned and looked at me. I knew his eyes were telling me to leave the freaking pigeons alone!

The birds followed me. I was happy that they did. They didn't know what was going on and they just wanted to have a snack. I stood at a distance and watched Yasser and Ihsan. Yasser whispered something in Ihsan's ear - something I couldn't hear. The pigeons were blobbing their heads in the background and making noises. They waited. They waited for someone to come. A few minutes later a new guy joined them and gave Ihsan a white envelope. He was apologetic. He was also big. Bigger than Ihsan and Yasser combined.

"Never do it again," Ihsan told him.

Then, hell happened. Ihsan punched the new guy. I saw the guy flying in the air and land heavily on the ground. Ihsan was wearing boots and he kicked the new guy in the face. Blood was splashing everywhere.

It felt like Ihsan was kicking a big bear that didn't really care. It was clear he was hurting. Ihsan thought he was done with the guy. Out of nowhere came another fellow like a shadow who attacked Ihsan from behind, knocking him to the ground. He was probably hiding somewhere and was waiting to come out, just in case things got nasty. After he knocked Ihsan to the ground, he knocked down Yasser too. The big guy was recovering, ready to attack. I thought I was next. I knew I was about to die. The big guy saw me and ran towards me. I was standing close to the edge this time and I knew that if he knocked me down, I would fall on the tracks. It all happened so fast. I didn't know how to react. As he was running towards me, I grabbed the pouch of seeds and threw it in the big guy's face. It blinded him. The seeds were scattered everywhere. In the blink of an eye, the pigeons joined in the fight. They attacked the guy's face, thinking it was food. Yasser jumped on him and knocked him down. Ihsan beat up the other guy. I stood there shaking. I had never been in such a situation before. Everything happened so fast.

"Run! Run!!" Yasser screamed as he ran down the stairs.

Ihsan ran in the other direction. I followed Yasser. I needed out. Our night didn't just end there. There was more to come.

***

"I'm Hitler's son!" screamed one of the kids riding on the train with us. Yasser had left his bike at the same spot. Those words came from a German kid harassing another Arab. Both cursed in German and Arabic. Yasser witnessed this. He was still heated, boiling from the previous fight. He didn't mind fighting again.

"No, Yasser!" I told him. "Don't do it!"

Yasser eyed the German kid. Everyone knew the kid was drunk, so drunk that I doubted he even knew what he was saying.

"You come to my country. Why? Go back to where you came from!" the German kid shouted. He swayed, unable to keep his balance. The girl next to him, probably his girlfriend, tried to get him to stop. She pulled his shirt. She was embarrassed. The kid was out of control. Yasser couldn't help it. The German kid tried to punch the Arab kid, but he missed his face. Yasser saw this and decided to join in. He punched the German kid in the face. The train was just about to stop. Yasser jumped out. I had nothing to do with it. But I had to follow Yasser everywhere he went. All I remembered was my feet hitting the ground hard and fast. We ran and we ran until we reached home.

"What the hell was that?" I asked Yasser. We were finally behind a locked door. In our house.

"It was nothing!" said Yasser.

"I go out for one night with you. We have one fight, and then another one. Are you trying to get us deported?"

I remembered the conversations I had with both Anna and Mr. Saleh. Keep away from trouble as much as possible. It's like they were psychics. Yasser lied and lied. Until I got him to talk.

He was selling drugs.

However, he promised me that this was the last time he was doing it to help a friend. I believed him, of course, with my super naivety. I believed him because I wanted to believe that this was the truth and that Yasser wouldn't do it again. Why wouldn't I believe him? He was my friend. I had to believe him.

***

There was a knock on the door and then another knock. I couldn't tell who could be visiting us this early in the morning. When I looked through the peep hole, I saw Mr. Saleh standing there. I opened the door and there he was, still wearing his jacket. Water droplets on the shoulders that still hadn't dried up.

"Good morning, sorry to bother you!" Mr. Saleh said. "Is your friend here?"

"My friend is still asleep," I said.

He told me not to worry. I told him how sorry I was that my friend had been rude to him the other day. I think Yasser overheard me saying that.

"Please tell him that I was looking for him. It's important."

Mr. Saleh was about to walk away. Then he turned around and gave me his business card. It read 'Mr. Saleh, pizzeria owner.'

I wouldn't be surprised if Mr. Saleh had looked up the refugee centre for new asylum seekers. The refugee centre was not far from the café anyway. Mr. Saleh did not want to talk about the reason he came. He didn't want to embarrass me or Yasser. But I knew he was looking for his wallet. He paused as he was walking away. Don't ask about it. Don't. Just go. I thought.

"I won't cause you any embarrassment. I'll just go."

After Mr. Saleh had left, I wondered if Yasser was awake and if he had heard the conversation. I heard him moving in bed. I closed the door. I looked at the business card. I thought about getting hold of the wallet and giving it back to its owner. Yasser wouldn't want to do the right thing.. Maybe I could steal it, I thought, but I didn't want to ruin my friendship with him. I sat there on my bed and I knew at that point that my friend was awake. I told him that Mr. Saleh had come by to apologise, and he wanted me to deliver his message.

"Do you believe this nonsense? He came for the wallet. He just didn't want to ask for it."

"Didn't you hear him?" I said.

"Why do you think he came?" asked Yasser.

"To apologise," I said.

"Come on, don't be naive! He's a liar. A preacher of morals!" said Yasser.

I thought about Yasser's words. He could have been right. I knew there was a reason why Mr. Saleh had come looking for the wallet: There was something more than the I.D cards and the money, there was something more important.

"Why do you think he's looking for the wallet?" asked Yasser.

"Why are you asking me? You have it!" I told Yasser.

Yasser searched the wallet. There was a picture of a woman. Mr. Saleh wanted the picture of this woman. That's why he had looked for us, found us and came all the way here. I wondered what the story of this picture was and why he would carry it in his wallet. Was she dead? Was she his wife? She could have been anyone. I left our room and took my thoughts with me.

I jumped on the train. I thought and pondered. I wondered. Upon arriving to the German class, I was distracted. Distanced. Zara talked and talked. Taught and taught. She could see I was absentminded. My mind was scattered across different train stations and faces I knew: Mr. Saleh, Anna, Ihsan and Yasser. My head was whirling. Looking at the ceiling. When I looked down, the class was finished.

"Are you going to spend the rest of the day here?" said Zara in a warm voice.

I looked up at her. I smiled when I saw her kind face.

"Are you okay today?" asked Zara.

I wondered if I should tell her about the trouble. I asked her out for dinner instead. She knew I was not the kind of person to ask her out, as if I had changed into something else, someone else overnight. When did I become so brave? How did I gathered enough courage to tell her I wanted to go out with her? And maybe tell her that I like her?

I went back home. Yasser was not there. I rushed to get dressed but I didn't have a shirt. I searched in Yasser's closet and took one of his nice white ones. I put it on fast. I had good reason to leave before he came back. I rushed out the door. But he was right there in my face. He asked me where I was going. I lied and said I was going to the library to study.

"Why are you so dressed up for the library?" Yasser asked me.

He could sense that I was lying, he was suspicious, but he didn't seem to notice I was wearing his shirt. Something blinded him that day. Or maybe he didn't want to make a big deal out of it. He already had his fair share of trouble, I guess.

At the Chinese restaurant, Zara and I sat facing each other. Our hands were stretched out on the table next to a candle. Her nails were so beautiful, painted red. We waited for the food to come.

"Why did you ask me to come?" asked Zara.

I didn't know what to answer. I wanted to tell her I had a crush on her, but it was too early. I wanted to tell her that I was in trouble, but I didn't want to scare her. I wanted to share something with her; I felt comfortable to share anything with her.

"Something happened last night...," I started talking.

"What happened?" asked Zara. But she was not ready to hear anything alarming.

I was struck by silence. I kept looking away and then back at her. Looking at her beautiful blue eyes and beautifully coloured nails. Red and radiant.

"Do you like the colour?"

Which colour? I thought. The colour of your eyes or your nails?

"Red colour," said Zara.

"I do, it brings a lot of memories."

"What kind of memories?" She asked.

"Red was the name of one of my favourite pigeons!"

I paused.

"Now she's dead."

Zara didn't know what to say. I didn't know either. The memory was reminiscent of a different past.

There are new memories that are created between the ones who leave. Zara held my hand to make me feel better. It was awkward. When she pulled her hand away, she saw my dirty nails and smiled. My dark and dirty black nails reminded me of who I was and all of a sudden, I realised how different and distant we both were.

I was not ready to talk about what had happened yesterday. I didn't want her to have a bad opinion of me. If I had told her, there would have been too much to explain and I wanted to enjoy my lunch and my time with her. There was the war, Yasser and so many other things I didn't want to talk about. It felt that if I started talking, it would take me back to the house; the one with the door which I had opened and closed. The one I had left. Once and for all.

The door of the restaurant opened. It was Yasser. Was he following me? Shit! Maybe he was coming for the shirt and knew that I had lied about going to the library. How the hell did he find me? So what! I didn't have to justify myself. He walked in and joined us with excitement. He pulled up a chair and introduced himself.

"I hope I'm not disturbing you guys. I came past the place and I saw you. I thought, why not say hi,"

"Are you studying?" asked Yasser.

"No, we were just having lunch. We're almost done," I said.

"Yes, can we get the bill?" asked Zara.

"Sure!" I ordered the bill.

Yasser sensed that we didn't want him to be there. He started acting up. He said he thought I was supposed to be at the library. How come the library had become the restaurant? I think he was trying to be funny. Zara continued our conversation as if Yasser was not there. That pissed him off even more. She started talking about Red, the pigeon.

Yasser spoke. "I remember that bird, the one you stole from our neighbour Abu Mahmoud..."

"What do you mean stole?" asked Zara.

Yasser felt he now had her attention. He started to backstab me and talk about my past as a pigeon whisperer in Syria. He told Zara that I was a pigeon thief, that I stole birds from the sky and claimed them to be mine. It was pure character assassination. I felt so angry. He ruined my moment with Zara. He told her that as a pigeon whisperer, our testimony in court was not accepted. He went on and on. Some of it was true, but why say it all now? I wanted him to stop. I didn't know what to do. I told Zara not to listen to him. She was becoming increasingly uncomfortable and clearly wanted to leave.

"Tell her who you are!" Yasser insisted.

"I will. I'm not ashamed of who I am." I said. "I will tell her everything."

I thought for a second. Took a deep breath. Looked at Zara in the eye and locked eyes with Yasser.

"Remember, Zara, what I started saying about last night? I have a friend who happened to be at the train station, and he saw something bad happen there…" I said.

Yasser turned pale. He kicked my leg from under the table. Zara listened attentively.

"Before I forget Yasser, do you still have my wallet with you?" I asked.

"Your wallet?" Yasser asked surprised.

Yasser didn't utter another word after that. The tension between him and I rose. He took Mr. Saleh's wallet out of his pocket, put it on the table and held onto it. He didn't release it, yet. I told him to give me back my wallet. He hesitated. I knew I was winning this time. Zara felt so awkward. She excused herself and asked if she could leave. Yasser was still holding onto the wallet. I pulled it out from under his hand. Zara said goodbye and left. I stared at Yasser. We heard the door close.

"I win this round!" I said.

"Asshole!" Yasser said.

I knew at this moment that this was the beginning of the erosion of our friendship- and the beginning of a new relationship, one of a different kind - maybe one that was not going to last, maybe one that would bring with it a lot of trouble.

I am the dead soldier. You might think I am dead, but I am alive in you. I fight for you. I am your mentor and protector; I am your shadow figure. I am your warrior. I am your dead soldier, don't ever leave me. I am alive in you and will always fight for you.

2
THE DEAD SOLDIER

I held the business card in my hand and felt my feet were leading me to Mr. Saleh's Pizzeria without a map or a guide. It was so easy to find. When I arrived, Mr. Saleh was sitting outside as if he had been waiting for me.

"I didn't expect you to come here." said Mr. Saleh.

Mr. Saleh ordered us a pizza and we ate and talked about life and Syria and the world and the war. I handed him his wallet. He asked me where I had found it and I told him I went back to the cafe and asked if anyone had handed it in. The cashier then gave it to me. Mr. Saleh knew I was lying. I could tell by the way he was looking at me. I had lied twice in a few days. I had lied to my friend and to Mr. Saleh. I had lied to myself. I had lied to the bird I took home without permission. I was starting to tell lies about myself – to myself- and everybody else. Maybe the pigeon lover and pigeon whisperer wasn't as pure-hearted and innocent as he had thought?

Mr. Saleh opened his wallet. Looked in it, to check if nothing was missing. His face turned pale, strange. His gaze fixated on the wallet, looking at an empty slot.

"Is there anything missing?" I asked.

Mr. Saleh didn't answer at first. He put the wallet on the table and showed me the blank slot where there once was a photo. At this point I knew Yasser took. Mr. Saleh took a deep breath. He started telling me about his family and how they meant everything to him. He explained how he had left the Arab world and that he didn't want to go back. He had left his whole life behind. I felt that we were similar in a way. We both left without looking back to be in a different world and live a different life.

"I don't know why I'm telling you all this. But you are like a son to me."

Mr. Saleh was not happy about the lost picture. He excused himself and left because he had a lot of work to do. He sat at a table with a computer, paper and a pen and started working. He was not the same person I had met a few minutes ago. It was as if he had just heard some terrible news or lost a part of himself – an irreplaceable part.

When I walked back home, Yasser was standing outside, leaning on his car puffing and looking away - into the distance. He pulled out another cigarette and smoked. He seemed worried and refused to tell me what was wrong. I felt tired and was ready for bed. When Yasser looked worried, it worried me too. As I prepared to enter the building, he stopped me. He told me to wait. At that specific moment, I wished I was a ghost. Invisible. A ghost to everything and everyone.

"Remember the trick you did last time with the birds?" he asked me.

"Which trick?"

"The one with the pigeons. When you threw the seeds at the guy," said Yasser.

Yasser walked closer to me, throwing his cigarette on the ground and stepping on it. I looked down at the cigarette butt for a second and imagined myself being that butt, being crushed under the weight of Yasser. It was too late to react. Yasser's last time and last promise was a lie. A fool is someone who believes fools, but what are you supposed to do when you have no other choice?

"Dabbour, do you think I would want to be deported? To go back to a place of no life? There is no return now. We are here now." Yasser said.

I was convinced. I believed Yasser. I had to believe him. He was my friend and friends believe each other. Don't they? Friends are expected to support each other in times of need, hardships and trouble. Friends are supposed to cover up each other's mistakes. I suddenly had a strange feeling we were being watched. There was someone standing on my shoulder like the angel of death watching and writing down notes. It could have been a camera or maybe Anna's eyes.

Maybe the whole world was watching me sink deeper into hell. I believed I could help Yasser. I wanted Yasser to swear on the Quran that he would't do it again. I was looking for a pigeon but there was not enough time. Then I remembered I had a pigeon in the apartment. The one I had hidden under the bed. The pigeon I had stolen from the Bellevue Bridge. Yasser didn't want to come with me to wherever he was assigning me to go. He slipped a note in my jacket and a plastic bag in my jeans. He warned me not to open the bag and then he left. I was all alone in this. I had to be smart and carry out the task my friend had assigned to me .

I reached into my pocket for the note which said that I was supposed to meet a guy at the train station at 12:00 a.m. He would be wearing a leather jacket. He wrote down the name of the subway station. I arrived there and there stood this guy on the other side of the platform. I was supposed to attach the small plastic bag to the pigeon's tiny feet. The big clock ticked, a few seconds before twelve. I could feel the sweat drip through my body despite the cold weather. The pigeon was sleeping inside my jacket. I unzipped it. I threw the seeds up in the air. My phone rang and it was the guy with the leather jacket.

"I can see you now. Give me a signal when you will fly the bird." he said to me.

Did I tell you that I actually marked her with blue tape to avoid any confusion? Despite my plans, the pigeon was uncooperative - she refused to fly. The seeds were not enough to seduce her and I was quickly running out of ideas. My mind was racing, I couldn't think of what else to do. My whole world turned blue and my thoughts went blank. All I could picture was Yasser staring at me, appalled that I had failed him. Then I remembered something.

I put my sweaty hands in my pocket and could feel something. It was the plastic bag I had used from when I flew the birds at Bellevue Bridge with Zara! It was my lucky day!

I pulled it out and waved it at the pigeon which was literally frozen near the edge of the platform. She was not moving; she was going to be hit by a train. I could hear it approaching in the distance. I knew that if I was not able to fly the pigeon in the next few seconds, I would lose her. I kept waving the plastic bag. It was making a loud sound but the bird still didn't want to fly. I then hit the bag so hard with a pole that it made a resonating noise that echoed through the entire station. The pigeon flew and landed on the guy's feet. The train arrived and I couldn't see what was happening on the other side. After it departed, the guy was gone. That's when I knew that the trick had worked.

Yasser thanked me and told me that I was a genius. I felt proud and bad simultaneously. Somehow, through all of this, I knew I was being watched. I knew I was a cheater, biting at the hands of those who were feeding me, protecting me. I felt bad. I knew I had betrayed my love for the birds and the life that had brought us together during all these years.

Walking with heavy steps towards home, I saw my world collapse before me. My perfect German dream and the European romantic streetlights all vanished. I no longer belonged here, no longer had a home. I was alone all over again.

***

There was no turning back. The road towards home was a long one and I thought that the road to Syria would be longer even if it was just a trip down memory lane. In my room, Yasser's voice was full of praise but faded away as he talked and talked.

"You are a genius man!" I heard him say.

How to escape now? How to tell Zara about all this? Why Zara? What would I tell Anna if she confronted me again? I would not be able to hide. I couldn't and didn't want to talk to anyone. I needed to be alone for days, months or years. I refused to leave the house; I was hiding away. I didn't want to see

Yasser; it was a relief he was gone during the day. If I wanted to leave the house, I dreaded to see Anna near the steps, peeking from the hole in the door. She would ask me questions that I would not be able to answer. You bit the hand that had welcomed you and let you in for safety. It made sense to tell Yasser to stop. He claimed that he was going to, but I wanted to tell him that I was out: I wanted out my friend.

That day, I passed by Mr. Saleh's pizzeria and decided to go in. Mr. Saleh smiled when he saw me and greeted me warmly. He offered me tea, but this time asked me to visit him at his house. I hesitated at first. I felt I needed a friend and some kind of reprimand. I made a promise to myself not to talk to him about what happened, so I went.

Mr. Saleh's house resembled a mini Syria. Handicrafts decorated the house. Picture frames. The smell of sage. I felt like I was entering a neighbourhood in old downtown Damascus similar to the Hamidiyah Souq. The same dried herbs and jasmine flowers which ornamented the stairs of our old house left to the test of time. Our childhood, innocence and hope: hope that had faded and had been lost and then reunited at the door of Mr. Saleh's apartment. I sat on his green couch and I could feel the slippery ground like the ocean waves, wet under my feet. Pictures spread across the living room. I heard the sound of boiling water from the kitchen. I imagined for a second that he was my dad. I heard his footsteps. Big glasses, genuine smile, slow talk and simplicity. When I talked to Mr. Saleh I felt like I had known him forever. I had to remind myself that real Syria was somewhere out there, not here. I was afraid of letting myself get attached to more illusions. I was done with emotional attachments. I didn't want anything to bring me back to the past.

We drank our tea and with every sip I felt the ground beneath me slip even further. Memories of the past that remained and lived in between the walls of this house. The wall talked back to me and wondered and gestured. Behind those walls, there was life and a future. The fear of looking into the future didn't equal to losing it. I wanted to remind myself that the past would always be the past. It would not last.

"Those without a past are those without a future." Mr. Saleh said. "I've been trying to throw its burden off my shoulders for a long time."

"I want to throw it behind me too". I said.

"You are still young Dabbour, you can! I'm old," said Mr. Saleh.

The recollection of memories and thoughts made it hard to get rid of the burden of the past across different generations. The quiet Berlin neighbourhood became a noisy one in my head as if I was in Cairo or

New Delhi; my head throbbing, hurting. The sage tea helped a little. The photos were ones of Mr. Saleh's deceased wife and the way he felt about it was unbelievable. He had her pictures everywhere. He must have felt regret about something. He couldn't do anything to bring her back and he felt hopeless. Mr. Saleh told me that his wife had never died in his heart, and never would.

"Never feel sorry for those who die. They remain with us and there's always something that they leave behind that keeps them alive in our hearts." Mr. Saleh said.

"What is it they keep with us?" I asked.

"Their spirit. It remains with us after they leave. People say it remains there for 40 nights." Mr. Saleh said.

"I heard that too." I said.

"That's wrong." said Mr. Saleh.

"Because technically their spirit roams around forever."

I told Mr. Saleh that I was not religious, and I didn't know much about these things. I preferred to be spiritual. Birds were my religion. The only religion I had ever known. I had no connection with any other. As we were talking, Mr. Saleh moved to the side of the couch and rested on the armchair looking away towards the light, watching the sun fading out.

"Their scent. Their presence. They keep their place and the space they occupy, always."

I didn't know what else to say. I was speechless. Mr. Saleh rested his hand on the armchair and looked away and closed his eyes and took a deep breath. There was a piece of cloth calligraphed on the armchair with his wife's name. Inscribed in Arabic: Noor. Noor meant light. Mr. Saleh lived for the memory of his wife. He lived for the memory of light, her light. I never asked him how she had passed away – I knew it would not make any difference. I listened to Mr. Saleh's words.

"I can still picture her sitting there. As if she had never left at all. She was light like a feather, my light, Noor." He said.

Mr. Saleh walked to the window and moved the curtain towards the light, towards her. There was still light, not so bright- hazy soft light. The dim lights lit the rest of the living room. Mr. Saleh started talking about guests that might arrive today. I felt scared. I thought Mr. Saleh was talking about angels – death. First, he talked about death and now guests. Somehow my mind associated both. I was confused. He told me to follow him and not to make any sound. He opened the door of the apartment and walked upstairs towards the roof.

Mr. Saleh opened the door to welcome his guests. Turns out they were guests that did exist. Mr. Saleh slowly peeked his head through the crack in the door, the wind blew in our faces. I heard sounds, familiar sounds. The sounds brought with them a thrill and a chill. I followed him upstairs. Mr. Saleh kneeled down and I thought he was praying, prostrating to his creator.

Mr. Saleh's visitors were pigeons. We watched them fly and disappear in the clouds.

"How often do they visit?" I asked.

"Their visits are random. One never knows when they'll come back again, but don't worry, they will come back."

Mr. Saleh's visit brought back a wave of nostalgia; memories I thought I had forgotten. One day, on the roof of our apartment, someone had slipped. I heard a sound. A scream. It was my brother. I wasn't there. The sound of this young boy's scream was so loud, I thought it would break the glass. The beam of light from his green eyes shined with the light of the sun. It beckoned me to come to his rescue. I ran upstairs and continued to run and run. When I got there, he was gone. He had fallen from the third floor and hit his head hard. He had bled a whole pool of blood. My younger brother was dead. Yasser was there too. He stood there, frozen like a statue. He was helping me with the birds. I later learnt that he had tried to give him a helping hand but had failed. It was too late. Yasser felt like a loser. He felt that he had betrayed our friendship. My friend didn't speak to anyone for a week. He started dreading everything. The only thing that made him talk after a week was the sound of drums of war urging him to run away, begging him to leave this place. I thought about what Mr. Saleh had mentioned about death. I thought it made sense. The dead might be dead to the world but to us they are not. They live in a different reality, parallel to ours. But then, this train of thought led me to think of someone dear to me and took me on a trip to the unknown.

That thought would never leave me. The thought of the rooftop and the pigeons occupying the sky, making it their ultimate home. I spent the next days thinking of my visit to Mr. Saleh's house. I walked past his house several times and looked at the rooftop. I thought about knocking on his door; I contemplated this idea a few times. Then I would walk away again, hoping that I would see signs of birds hovering above his rooftop.

There were times I would wish this mental torture would end and every time I walked down the stairs to catch the train, I would imagine seeing a familiar face. I saw ghosts and lovers, shadows and feathers reflecting on the walls of the old train station and the written dates on the walls, old, like timelines and excerpts of history and reoccurring memories vanishing and then showing up again. Like a fading light to remind us of who we are and what we are and what has become of us. Where we are didn't matter anymore. The time we are living in is always changing. The words we are speaking are similar to whispers which can no longer be heard; they are barely spoken, remaining inside the wounds hoping to heal themselves with time.

I was aware that I had promised myself not to be lured by Yasser anymore and not to follow his steps wherever he went. But I kept finding myself being pulled between him and his friends, as if caught in a game of tug of war. Each of us was pulling harder, attempting to win. Yasser's force was stronger. He possessed the right combination of charm and reason to drag me into his dark world. At this point in my life, I felt there was no point looking towards the light anymore – towards the good side of things. Towards hope.

Tonight was just another night of suffering and feeling lonely, chasing the shadows in my mind. The feeling of being tracked down by the shadows, coyotes and dogs in the subways of the Berlin that scared the hell out of me, and other times loved me. Like restrained and captivated lovers who are shy or maybe do not know how to love yet - love forgotten, love abandoned.

I felt lost and found myself sitting next to Yasser again in his car going somewhere - to an unknown location. The destiny always remained unknown.

"Where are we going? And whose car is this?" I asked Yasser. He remained silent. His silence killed me and penetrated the tiny piece of sanity that was left in me. Yasser had now bought a car.

He was scared but seemed happy to be making enough money to buy a car. I was not sure if he felt regret or if he was mulling the situation he had purposely put himself in. Maybe he was involved in this mess because he had been forced or had felt threatened, had he decided to retreat at some point. He had even admitted it in a trembling and shaky voice.

"I can't!" Yasser said.

I was also trying to remind myself of where I was deliberately leading my life to. I wanted to leave the car. I was boiling inside. I unbuckled the car seat and tried to open the door and get out.

"Why can't you?" I asked Yasser before I walked out of the car.

He looked at me and grabbed my collar, eyes shining from the streetlight like a ghost.

"You have to decide now Dabbour!"

"Decide what?" I asked.

"Are you in or out?" asked Yasser.

I wanted to trust Yasser and help him out of this. I wanted to say no and walk away, walk home and never see him again. I wanted to tell Yasser to retreat or he would have to retrace his steps back home where he didn't belong anymore.

"The police..." I said thinking if I should tell him about Anna or forget about it. But his madness, similar to that of a raging bull, made me rethink my next move. He tugged at my collar again. I could feel him pulling more and more. It hurt and I could feel the sore pressure on my neck.

"What did you say to the police?" Yasser said raging.

"Nothing, nothing, believe me!"

"I believe you this time!" said Yasser.

I think he forgot the word "not". I could see his eyes reflecting mistrust. I shut my mouth the whole night observing and thinking of what I had gotten myself into.

"I knew it! I knew it!" Zara said when I told her about what had happened. She told me about a visit she had from a police officer who had asked her about me and my friends. Zara knew Yasser was involved into something awful and she told me to stay away from him. How could I keep a safe distance when I lived with him in the same room? The police must have been tracing his phone calls by now. Like coyotes, they were hiding in their caves waiting for the right moment to attack.

I had promised Yasser to help him tonight but I needed to find a way to run away and out of this mess. I had an idea. I would teach Yasser how to fly the birds. Maybe if I did, he would let me go and I would be left alone forever. My phone rang. It was Mr. Saleh. He asked me if I was free. He told me he wanted to discuss an important matter with me. I told him I was available the next day.

We sat on Mr. Saleh's porch barely speaking, just looking at the passersby, bikers, and walkers.

"So, did they visit again?" I asked, trying to break the silence.

"They might have, let's go and see," said Mr. Saleh

We put on our coats and walked upstairs. It was damn cold. I felt we would need blankets on top of our jackets. The tea in our hands had become cold and the birds never came.

"That's strange that the birds haven't visited for a while. They must be sensing danger," Mr. Saleh said.

I was not sure if Mr. Saleh was hinting at something or maybe he was a psychic? Maybe the birds felt heartbroken, betrayed? I felt doubt and paranoia. I had feelings of guilt. Splits of amnesia and heartache. Even the birds knew it and I felt unwelcome – they didn't want to be in my presence.

"I think it's going to rain tonight, some heavy rain according to the weather forecast...," said Mr. Saleh. "Look at the clouds too."

The clouds and another topic that Mr. Saleh was not done with felt compatible. Mr. Saleh asked me why I had lied about the wallet. He knew I had not found it in the café. He knew everything. He was the man with the godly hand after all. I wondered if he knew where my destiny was going to lead me. I wondered if he knew what kind of birds my life was going to breed.

"I went to the café before you and I didn't find any wallet!"

Mr. Saleh hated lies and liars and I told him that I didn't lie. I didn't want to lie. He told me that he was not accusing me and he knew who had taken the wallet. That I shouldn't keep covering up for my friend's mistakes. He advised me to look out for myself and be careful. Mr. Saleh knew that Yasser had taken his wallet and stolen his wife's picture. Then he told me that it was not my fault and that I needed to watch my back. I couldn't utter a word. My tongue was tied.

"Listen, whatever you are hiding, I don't care, just be careful! I want you to be careful," Mr. Saleh said.

The rain started pouring down heavily and Mr. Saleh told me something that I thought I had misheard due to the noise of the rain falling with force – so I ignored it. But when I heard it again, I knew instantly that I hadn't misheard anything the first time.

After a few minutes, the rain stopped and we could hear each other again. We walked back inside the house, and out of nowhere Mr. Saleh offered me a business opportunity. He offered me a chance to find home and hope again.

"I want to offer you a chance to breed your pigeons again...," said Mr. Saleh.

I didn't understand what Mr. Saleh meant at first but then he explained.

"I will give you the money to buy the birds. You will breed them. We share the profits. Deal?" said Mr. Saleh.

It was the perfect business deal. I didn't know how to thank my new friend. I was still in denial. I could not believe this was happening. We shook hands. I left his house. I called Zara to tell her. Maybe she was asleep or preparing to sleep but I didn't care. I didn't want to wait for the morning to tell her the news. I was excited. When she picked up the phone, she was scared; she thought I had bad news for her.

"You scared the shit out of me! I thought something bad had happened to you!" said Zara.

I told Zara about the deal. She was half asleep.

It was Friday night and there was no work and no classes the next day. The Germans took both their weekends and their weekdays seriously. The house was German-styled, one that I had dreamt about before, warm lights and streetlights blending together. It was nice and orderly. It had Zara's very distinctive scent. I felt like I had dreamt of this house many times before and dreamt of her too, maybe in a different world. I could not believe she had told me to come or that I had the guts to say yes. We were friends, I thought. Good friends. She made me coffee. Zara loved coffee and we talked for so many hours and we stood onto her balcony staring into the sky. Everyone was drinking, that's what Germans did on the weekend. We hoped to join a conversation with a person passing by so they could join us too. She could tell I was worried. She could not tell why though. She thought I felt shy. Forgetting why I came here in the first place. The feeling of being lost which seemed to be a recurring life pattern for me. I thought we were supposed to celebrate tonight. That was our kind of celebration: healing.

"I have to tell you something, Dabbour," she said to me. Zara sounded serious.

I told Zara that I had to tell something to tell her too. She told me to go first. She was shocked when I told her that I had helped Yasser with something. I had no justification other than admitting that I was wrong. I promised her that I would figure something out and escape from his grasp. I made her a promise. Zara looked away.

"What did you want to tell me?" I asked her.

She told me to forget about it. She was not in the mood for it, but I insisted.

"Are you sure?" she asked.

"Yes, please." I insisted.

"Dabbour, we're not what you think we are!" she said.

I wish I hadn't asked her to say more. She told me that we were just friends. Sometimes the feelings unsaid are better. They hurt less. She broke my heart with what she said. But her apology made it even worse. Like I was pathetic, desperate and hopeless.

"Is that why you said yes to me visiting you?" I asked.

She nodded. I felt fooled. I left the house without even finishing the coffee. I wanted to weep. It's hard to weep when you don't know what you are weeping for. I felt swept up in shame and regret for even opening up to her. But I should have known better. Now I could at least walk home and admit it to myself, that perhaps it was a foolish idea to love her or even like her. I called Yasser but he didn't answer. I called him again. I didn't want to go home. I wanted to exit the

Yasser game as well. I felt it was only a matter of time before he would get caught. Only a matter of time.

**

I knew where Yasser was. Without much thought I went there, to the Arab street in Berlin. He was there with his friends. They seemed more like a gang to me. They called themselves "Al Shilleh", literally the gang. They gathered around each other smoking Hookah, laughing and playing cards. They somehow managed to distract themselves from everything happening in the world, including the war in their own country and their fragile situation. That was the way they coped. They knew they couldn't carry the weight of the world forever. It was their coping mechanism against depression and tragedy. I walked towards their table. Yasser saw me from across the room and his face turned pale. He saw how scared I was, like a bird shrinking from the rain. He left the table and walked with me outside.

"What's wrong? Why did you come here?" Yasser asked me.

"I called you. Why didn't you pick up the phone?" I asked Yasser.

Yasser asked me why I had called him. He was suspicious that I could have done something wrong. He wanted me to go home. I was obviously an embarrassment to him in front of his friends. He asked me to go home again. I had to spit the words out and go. I wanted Yasser to know I was out. That I could no longer help him. But I wanted an assurance that we would still be friends. I promised him that I would be ready to help him with anything, but not in smuggling drugs. Yasser knew I was hurt. I told him that I had broken up with Zara. He felt happy for me because he knew that she and I were not together anyway, which meant that I needed to stop being delusional.

"I feel bad Yasser. I want to start a new chapter. Please!"

"Man, I told you. Zara never liked you. She's out of your league anyway. I am happy it is over between you two," Yasser said bluntly. "Before it has even started!"

"She will love me when I am successful and have money." I said.

"What are you trying to say?" asked Yasser.

"I am trying to say that you should do the same. Follow your dream. Didn't you always want to work at a German car company? Mercedes? BMW?" I asked.

Yasser laughed. "That was in ancient times, my friend. How are you going to make money, then? I don't understand." Then he whispered, "Are you selling drugs?"

"No, no. I made a deal with Mr. Saleh to buy pigeons, raise them and sell them. It's a 50/50 partnership." I said.

It was a big mistake to tell Yasser about the deal and that there was money involved. Yasser felt insecure and knew that I would not need him anymore. He also realised that if this deal worked, I would be out of his life forever.

"But we're still friends. Right, Yasser?" I said.

Friends? For the first time I felt I had the power to control him. I was still feeling hurt from the loss of Zara, but I felt I was regaining control over something else. That made me feel better. For God's sake, what are friends? What were friends made for? With the current ticking of time and passage of life, things were confused, lost. I kept reflecting on friendship and lost relationships.

The streets spread and stretched widely as I headed back home. I wanted to lose my way and be late in reaching home. I erred in different alleys and different streets. It was spontaneous but refreshing. Walking, just walking aimlessly. Yasser made it home before me. He locked the door from inside. I knocked once; there was no response. I looked and saw all my stuff was thrown outside in the hallway. Yasser was sending me a message: to go to hell and find somewhere else to live. Yasser was paying rent from the money he had made selling his dad's car. That car was the stolen gift that kept paying back. The bird cage I made was also thrown in the hallway and the pigeons' nest was destroyed. All my stuff was upside down. Ironically, my whole life had been turned downside up. I knocked harder and harder, forgetting how late it was. A neighbour opened the door to his house and told me that she was going to call the police if I didn't stop or leave. She said I was disturbing the whole building. I apologised. I didn't know where to go. I thought I had no place to go except Mr. Saleh's house. I thought it was a bad idea to call him at this time. I decided to go anyway and tell him what had happened. At least he was someone who cared: I hoped I wouldn't sleep on the street. I didn't want to.

I found myself looking at the front of Mr. Saleh's house. I glanced up and saw the light still on in his living room. Although it was dim, he must still be awake. I was past caring anyway; I was tired and scared. I walked up to the front door and knocked softly.

Mr. Saleh opened the door and welcomed me. He looked pale. I apologised for waking him up. Mr. Saleh told me to come in. I told him that I had a fight with Yasser and that he had kicked me out of the house. Mr. Saleh was happy that Yasser had done what he had done to get rid of me. He told me I could sleep in his house until my situation was sorted out.

"Why do you think your friend has changed?" asked Mr. Saleh.

I told him that I wasn't sure. He knew that I knew. Everything. Mr. Saleh went to his bedroom and came back with an envelope. He told me that this was the money for the birds, and that I could start buying them first thing in the morning.

"Mr. Saleh, I need a place to sleep."

"You can stay here until you find a place," Mr. Saleh said again.

Either I stayed there or I would have to choose the street, I realised. I didn't know what to say or how to thank Mr. Saleh.

He excused himself to make some tea. I heard the water boiling and all of a sudden there was no movement. I waited and waited, and everything was quiet. I waited for a sound again. The tea was over-boiling and the time shattered. I forgot myself on the couch and I thought I snoozed a little, a minute or two. I looked at the time and I realised it had been fifteen minutes. I peeked into the kitchen, but I didn't see Mr. Saleh. He had never walked into the living room: he was still there in the kitchen, lying on the floor not moving, body stiff. Mr. Saleh had collapsed. I didn't know what to do. I shook him and tried to wake him up. His hands were cold. I tried to breathe into his mouth, but he wouldn't respond. I ran to the living room and picked up the phone. I was shaking. My world was spinning around.

I tried to call Zara. She was the first person I thought of calling. Maybe because she was buried in the back of my head and in my soul. She never answered. The phone rang and rang with no answer. I dialled Anna's number. I still remembered how she told me to call her if I needed anything. I am glad I remembered. Anna answered. Trouble. That's what she responds to. I wanted to tell her what had happened. I stuttered. I got scared that if I said anything it would be used against me. I didn't know what to say or what to tell her. As soon as I heard her voice, I hung up the phone.

I called Yasser; he was the only one who could help me.

"Yasser, come to Mr. Saleh's house!" And I gave him the address. I paused. "Mr. Saleh is dead. Come now, please."

I dropped the phone and I tried to revive Mr. Saleh again. He was stiff and cold. He just wouldn't wake up.

"Mr. Saleh!" I screamed again.

I was not sure how long it took Yasser to come but I knew he was on the way. Sometimes when you live in hell, you lose track of time. Like the saying that hell lasts for eternity. That's what eternity was. Minutes later, I heard footsteps coming up the stairs, climbing fast. But Yasser was not alone. He was with Ihsan. They had come to the rescue. Short of breath, I pointed to the kitchen, still shaking. I stood there frozen and then I heard the noise ease and the whole house turned into another kind of silence, a creepy silence. Mr. Saleh was officially dead.

The world. Oh, how I loved the world and hated it at the same time. Life always surprised me and still does, with its unexpected occurrences. Sometimes it would feel like a smooth ride on a highway. At other times, it would feel like ink on paper slowly fading out with time. The words written on paper smudged by your hands. You can no longer make sense of the words.

Mr. Saleh's heart had stopped beating. He was still lying on the kitchen floor. I felt out of breath because he was breathless. The oxygen in the house was running short. The three of us sat in the living room on Mr. Saleh's couch. I went to the kitchen to pick up my phone from the floor and I tried to call the ambulance. There was a man dead and that was the most logical thing to do – maybe not for Yasser and the others. They perceived the situation very differently.

Ihsan snatched the phone from my hand and tried to calm me down by firmly pushing me back on the couch every time I would stand up. Every time I would try to stand up he would push me down and sit me down again.

"Who are you calling?" Ihsan asked me.

I was calling the ambulance, I told him. The two of them standing in the room stared at me as if I was crazy.

"Do you really want to call the ambulance?" Yasser asked me in a hushed voice.

"There's a dead man on the kitchen floor, we need help," I said.

Yasser was about to speak but Ihsan shushed him and, with a low trembling voice, he said

"Okay, let's call the ambulance." "I will call the ambulance."

We all thought he was joking. He was serious. Dead serious. Ihsan never joked. I never saw him joke or even smile. He dialled the number and I could hear the phone ringing on the other side. Then I heard the voice of the coroner respond. As soon as he heard it, Ihsan moved the phone to my ear, still holding it in his hand for me to talk.

"What's your emergency?" The coroner said, his voice vibrating through the phone line.

Ihsan gestured to me, urging me to talk. I was shaking. I didn't know whether I was doing the right thing or the wrong thing.

"I would like to report an incident," I answered.

There was a pause. Ihsan looked at me with a penetrating stare.

"Tell him. Come on," Ihsan whispered in my ear. I was paralysed.

"Tell him what happened," said Ihsan again.

"A man has dropped dead. He had a heart attack," I said. "We need urgent help."

"Where is your location?" The coroner asked.

It was that moment. The world started closing in on me and I started seeing what Ihsan was trying to do. I heard the police sirens approaching. I saw the lights of the ambulance, red and blue, dancing in Mr. Saleh's warm and cozy apartment, turning it into an investigation scene, a crime scene. Police buzzing in the house like bees in a hive. I could hear the bang of the door of the building opening and the footsteps of the ambulance staff and the police storming in. I heard the tea pot on the stove. Water no longer boiling, cold like Mr. Saleh's hands, cold like the stagnating blood in his body, cold like my nights and dreams.

"We never drank our tea," I told the coroner through the phone lines.

"What? What's your location? Where is it?" the voice repeated over the phone.

"Don't tell him," Ihsan whispered in my other ear, going around me in circles like the devil. If you tell him, all of us will be sent back to Syria. We're all in it together. The drug smuggling. Everything…" Ihsan said.

Ihsan would just go on and on.

"The police. The cameras. If you tell him where we are, it's all over buddy - the German dream and the hope of a future - any future."

Ihsan was giving me a speech and the coroner was still waiting on the phone line. I could hear Ihsan's words. I could even feel the coroner's breath through the speaker. I imagined his fingers on the keyboard, ready to type in the location. Ihsan continued.

"Syria is no longer the Syria we once knew. The Syria that you knew is gone."

Ihsan's voice echoed in my head and I remembered Mr. Saleh was now dead.

"I can't say. I'm sorry." And I hung up.

The guys heaved a sigh of relief and I could see them smile. The sigh of relief did not have a long-lasting effect because there was a dead body we had to deal with.

"What do we do now?" I asked.

"Let's have some tea!" said Ihsan. Everyone looked at him like he was crazy. I didn't think he was crazy at all. I knew why he said that. He was reading my mind.

"But the tea is cold." I said.

"No problem. We'll reheat it."

Ihsan gestured to Yasser and he ran to the kitchen to boil the water again. Making tea while there was a dead body on the kitchen floor? Being careful not to step over it like someone walking in a cemetery. I was still in denial. Yasser brought the tea and he stared at the tea pot refusing to drink form it. I did. Ihsan did. This was my way of saying my last goodbye to the friend who had saved my life once. To the person who briefly taught me how to not break the rules and to abide by the law. But all the paths were now dead ends. All dreams had just vanished. There was no way of looking forward and seeing the light again. It was dark that night and getting darker.

"We never drank our tea...," I found myself muttering again.

We never got to drink our tea; the tea which was supposed to warm our hearts. Life was so unpredictably scary; one minute your teapot is boiling and the next minute you were mourning the death of someone you love and respect. I was talking about life and of new beginnings, and now, today and tomorrow all I can think about is death. There were no words to express any feeling; to remember nothing at all was a blessing. To remember something would take me back to my childhood. To remember innocence - if it had existed at all, if it ever did exist or if it ever will. To remember nothing at all is a blessing. To dive into the random memory and recall, call my name and the names of those I love and have loved me - whether they were here, gone, or almost there. To call and hear the echoes of their voices calling back your name.

"Dabbour...," Yasser told me. "We need your help."

I looked at Yasser with my sad bewildered eyes.

"What are we going to do?" I asked.

"We're going to the woods…" said Yasser.

"Woods?"

"To bury the body!" said Ihsan.

***

I am the horse that runs. I am the loyal, the confused, the wounded one. I am the horse, lost is my home but eventually I find my way to somewhere, to anywhere. I run and run despite my wounds. I finish the race and I don't come first. But for me, this is my victory.

3
THE WOUNDED HORSE

I felt my heart sink even more as we carried Mr. Saleh and wrapped his body in a carpet. How did this even happen? When did this happen? Isn't it terrible to bury your friend? You might ask. Wouldn't it be terrible if the dead were to wake up and ask what had happened? Was it the end of the world? Did anything even matter, in the end? If Mr. Saleh woke up and asked me where he was, what would I tell him? Where was I taking him? If he asked me why he was being thrown in the trunk of a car, how would I answer him? This was not what Mr. Saleh wanted. My heart sunk to my feet when I remembered that he was forever dead – and I was on my way to bury him.

I stood there by the door as Yasser and the guys wrapped Mr. Saleh in his own rug, like a baby wrapped in a blanket. He looked as if he was sleeping in peace. We could have called the ambulance and ran away; we could have called the police and just disappeared. Fingerprints were all over the house, on the table, smudged on teacups, all over the kitchen surfaces and everything else. On the doorknobs, on the curtains, on the lamps, on the shades of grey and the shadows of ghosts roaming around the house.

"Are you going to help or just stand there staring?" Yasser said.

I grabbed a cloth and started cleaning the surfaces like a professional. The staircase was clear for us to smuggle the body down. I whispered to Yasser and kept guard on the way down. It was like sliding down the staircase to an unknown land of ghosts, death angels and floating spirits. We were in a rush and I found myself sitting behind the steering wheel, driving us to the woods - driving us towards hell. You know you are on your way to that dark place when the high towering streetlights become demons and the clouds hover over your head and eye you menacingly. Ihsan sat in the front seat in his own car, giving orders and setting directions to inflict more misery. He handed me the car keys and told me to drive.

"Head to the woods." He said.

I froze behind the steering wheel, unwilling to believe what had just happened. Mr. Saleh was done dying right there, just like we were done living in that exact moment. A few minutes later, my phone rang and I was startled by the vibration. The call scared me. I answered by mistake because my hands were trembling. I tried hard to hide my nervousness from Ihsan and the guys. There was no time for grief. I wanted to grieve. Grievances happen in strange times – in order that the pain does not kill us. There was silence and a deep breath that sucked all the air left in the car. I decided to answer to try and clear any doubt that the caller might have regarding what was wrong. I gathered my courage and said hello. Anna was on the other side. I tried to cut the call short for I didn't want Ihsan to know I was in touch with the authorities.

"Your voice is trembling; are you in trouble?" asked Anna.

"I'm okay," I said. "Can I call you later? I'm in the middle of something."

"Are you sure?" Anna asked.

"Yes, I'm sure!" I said.

"Call me if you need anything." Anna said.

"I will." I said.

I won't, I said to myself. What do you want me to tell you? It was a crazy idea to call you, Anna. It's already crazy to fall from a height but when you are already falling and can't go back, you find yourself stuck in a vicious cycle. The car drove a few kilometres and we stopped at a traffic light. Ihsan pulled the handbrake and stopped the car from moving forward. The traffic light was green. The car behind us honked but we didn't move. Ihsan insisted on sharing a couple of words with me.

"Dabbour, I just want to make something clear to you. From this moment on, we are all in this together. We are one. There's no turning back. Understand?"

That day was the day I knew. I had lost the ability to make decisions about my own destiny. I had lost the freedom to be my true self. From this moment on, I knew that these sinister guys were part of my new tribe. I was going to protect them, protect myself from them and them from me. I knew that Yasser was swimming in muddy waters too and he was very keen to drag me along with him. Maybe because he liked me, and I was his friend. When you like your friend, you want to take them with you wherever you go, don't you? Even if it meant taking them to hellfire. I wanted to help Yasser, but I knew I wanted to help myself too. It was time for me to start thinking things through. I had to learn how to swim too. I had to learn how to survive unexposed and unharmed in the heat of the blazing fire. But how? I was already deep into it. I knew that if I dived further into the fire, or if anyone else did in fact, we would all free-fall together: all of us. Together.

Ihsan, a man of religiously wrong beliefs with a slightly long beard and a bunch of grey hair, was willing to do anything to protect those who bowed down to him and made him feel worthy of trust. He was seemingly so afraid of committing sins that he ended up committing all sorts of wrongs. His sins were his demons. Demons which totally controlled him. He deliberately mistreated us in an attempt to protect himself from his self-loathing. The truth was that he was a piece of shit. And he knew it. We knew it. To him, I was too odd, too strange, unappealing. But the reality was that his whole persona was off-putting to all of us. He actually scared the hell out of us. We were so stupid to think that he was capable of anything. What a strange turn of events that was. Here I was, driving someone else's car to the woods in order to bury the man who had considered me like his son and wanted to help me out of my misery. Ihsan was about to take Mr. Saleh's place in that regard– forever.

The birds! A voice inside of me screamed out. I found myself blaming the birds for everything and I felt contempt for them. I was beginning to blame them for everything. Damn them. They had lured me into a trap. And now look at me. I wished I had never jumped in front of that train, I wished I had never met Mr. Saleh. I wished I had never listened to Yasser. Perhaps, then, things would have been different? Maybe Mr. Saleh would have died alone in his apartment and none of this would have happened, none of it. This strange love for the pigeons was turning sour and I could feel it burn my soul and ache my heart like a slit, oozing wound.

Hands on the steering wheel, driving through the hazy and blurred street lights, the carpet rumbling at the back of the trunk. Deep inside those German woods, there was nobody. This is where we were heading to get rid of the body. There was a corpse about to be buried into the ground. Hands in the mud, deeply immersed in the life or the idea of life that was awaiting me.

"Help me!" I cried out loud, but they just stood there watching me with blame making me feel more shame.

I felt their eyes looking at me like wolves in the night. Red eyes. I felt shame. And I could feel the weight of their blame weighing down on me. They told me that he was my friend and because he was my friend, they were not going to help me. I was to bury him alone while they waited in the car. But I was not a killer. I was not a murderer. I had nothing to do with this. They wanted every part of my body and mind to be immersed in this. They wanted me to commit to this crime with a murderous passion. They wanted to make sure that there was no turning back. Their evil selves wanted to ensure that they could use me for everything they wished for. I had fled Syria because I didn't want to have to bury my pigeons, but look at me now. Soaked in mud, with a shovel in my hand in the middle of the night, burying Mr. Saleh. Had I been cursed?

I dug my benefactor's grave. After a few hours of digging, I felt completely exhausted. Emotionally drained. I could see the light shining on the horizon, the sun rising. After removing the carpet which revealed a part of Mr Saleh's face, I looked at my friend one last time and I said goodbye. Memories flooded in. I could recall myself asking him about the wallet, his voice echoing in the background. I patted the back of my pocket and his wallet was here. I must have picked it up while I was cleaning the surfaces in his house. I paused for a few seconds and I contemplated the empty slot. Mr. Saleh was so preoccupied with that empty slot and I wish I could have done something about it. I wish I could have brought his wife back to life, become Jesus and raise her from the dead. I wish I could have saved them both. If I could turn back time, I would not have been to the café with Mr Saleh and he would not have lost his wallet. And his wallet would not have been in my hand right now digging while I was digging his grave. I put the wallet back in my pocket and I apologised to my old friend. I told him we were running out of time and I promised him that one day I would explain everything to him.

Everything had changed in a split second. I felt alone all over again. Things were about to get ugly - really ugly. Yasser's voice whispered from behind me and he woke me up from my nightmare only to assure me that this terrible living dream was not over yet.

"Everything is going to be okay Dabbour…" Yasser said to me, putting his hand on my shoulder. "Things are going to be okay."

Yasser's hand on my shoulder felt cold and the distance between us, as we headed home, was growing. The contrast was stark and the separation utterly painful. It felt like we were two birds of the same flock, doing everything together. We would come and go together. Birds of the same flock love each other. If they hurt each other, they would forgive each other. If they bled together, they would heal each other's wounds. Birds of the same flock could also speed up their race with karma and towards their demise, towards their final destiny. We were like birds, we thought we knew each other. But we were mere strangers, parting, celebrating and dancing in our own unique way.

That night, I thought long and deep about what to do with the money. Burn it maybe? Hide it? Or throw it in the river? I knew that if Yasser found the money, he would find a way to spend it and definitely not in a way Mr. Saleh or I wished to do so. The money was a burden on my shoulders, and I didn't know what to do with it. I found myself lying on my bed and Yasser was deep asleep, entangled in his bittersweet nightmares. I paced the streets and waited for the new day to come, a fresh light, looking for some hope, any sign of hope.

I wanted to complete the task that Mr. Saleh had assigned to me. I wanted to start buying birds but I didn't know where to find them. I looked around and found myself peeking inside a pet shop, but it was too early in the morning. The pet shop was closed. I wondered if everything that had happened last night was a dream. I was hoping Mr. Saleh would appear any second to open his restaurant. I looked there and I thought I saw him, like a silhouette figure passing by. There he was. I stood there and everything changed, time was reversed. I heard the echoes of his voice. At least he knew how the grip on reality had been lost along the way. My entire reality and love for the birds had unfolded into yet another tragedy. I picked up the envelope, held the money in my hand and walked around the city, hoping to find a place where I could buy pigeons – I found none.

As I was starting to despair, a miracle happened. As if a new star had just been born in the Berlin pigeon sky. A man in his eighties, with bald hair and a long white beard, opened the door of his van. His vehicle was a caravan for pigeons of all kinds. I stopped abruptly, as if unable to believe what my eyes had just seen. I thought about approaching the man and talking to him. But he wouldn't even look at me or talk to me. He just ignored me. He sat on the edge of the van and started feeding his pigeons. I had an instant flashback of myself standing at the Turkish border again. There was a resemblance of imprisonment and I had the urge to set those birds free. I wanted to be in this man's place. I wanted to be him so much. I wanted to be old and live with the pigeons. It didn't matter where or when, the tiny space was enough, more than enough. I could feel that these birds were happy. And this realisation highlighted the fact that I was unhappy without them. I lost myself in time but then, one of the pigeons' sparkling eyes caught my attention. I walked closer to the van; I wanted to verify the acuity of my own vision. I couldn't believe what I was seeing. There she was, sitting in the back of the van, gracious like a queen. I instantly fell in love with her. I had fallen in love with her a long time ago. She was the rarest pigeon in the world, the Armando pigeon. I thought I was daydreaming. The very sight of her seemed unreal. The old man grew increasingly suspicious. I had to walk away. I had to take a step back, but I knew he was still looking at me. The old man knew. He knew that I knew. He closed the door of the van. I wondered if he was aware of how rare that pigeon was. I decided to approach him and initiate a conversation.

"Can I help you?" the old man said to me.

"No thank you! I'm just impressed with your van and the birds." I said.

"Thank you, they are not for sale, please walk away." The old man said.

"I couldn't help but notice the Armando Pigeon." I said.

He was surprised. And suspicious of me. He knew that I knew: it was a rare pigeon, priceless, a half million Euros? Maybe more. She was every pigeon breeder's dream – an undeniably unattainable dream for me. I wondered how he had acquired the bird; had it been gifted to him? She was one of ten in the world. She was the queen of all pigeons. I bowed to her and left.

I walked out of sight and the sparkle of the pigeon's eye would not fade out, lighting my way like a flashlight in the darkness. I imagined that I did a magic trick and made her disappear from the van and reappear into the inside of my jacket. I kept her warm from the bitter cold. Her eyes and Zara's eyes blended together. Love was one. Love anywhere on earth shared the same characteristics. It felt the same everywhere we went.

The news of Mr. Saleh's death spread across town very fast. I called Yasser on the way out in an attempt to halt his movements or any suspicious plans until things had calmed down again. He was not worried. He was in complete denial. He had consciously led himself to believe and act as if nothing wrong had happened. He was trying to behave as if everything was going to be alright. Yasser asked me to meet him at a nearby café – the street that started to get busy before the weekend.

"Be careful! Slow down, we are being watched," I told Yasser.

"I have no idea what you are talking about!" said Yasser, looking around, his eyes scanning around the café.

"Yasser pulled me outside. In a muffled voice, he told me not to ever mention or even remember what had happened.

"Do you understand me?" Yasser said.

I was about to walk away but I felt the pull from my arm. Yasser warned me not to ask any questions and to meet him tonight. He wanted me to steal some birds. I knew I had no other choice. That night, Yasser gave me his gym bag and dropped me at the Berlin underground station and told me to go and catch some birds.

"Catch some birds?" I asked.

"Yes, and try not to get caught," Yasser said.

There were cameras everywhere and police officers walking by. I had to pretend that I was just a nobody walking there waiting for the train, any train. I traced the birds as they tried to hide from me, behind the poles, up the stairs, near the rushing feet of passengers eager to get home. I walked as slowly as I could. When I realised that I was in the blind spot of the cameras, I dropped some seeds on the ground. The birds trusted me. They liked me. I thought about the Germans as people who were taught to trust; they even taught their birds to be as trusting. The sense of trust and responsibility. Similar to when you try to ride on a train and never buy a ticket. You feel so small, so little. Even when you don't get caught, the feeling is still here: you still feel bad. The birds felt at home there, trusting that no one was going to hurt or steal them - why would anyone harm them? I was purposely there to disrupt their inner peace. I was about to turn their tranquil life into utter chaos.

I walked out of the train station and onto the street. There was a guy sitting there on his old rug playing his flute. On the opposite side, there was a bakery. I could smell the freshly baked bread and the freshly-brewed coffee. I heard a sound. I saw a shadow mimicking my footsteps, following me everywhere I went. I refused to look back. I headed straight to the door. I wanted an escape. I was hungry and wanted to stop at the bakery, but I didn't. I couldn't. What if someone was following me? I realised that there was no point hiding anymore. I stopped and looked back. I was being followed by my own shadow. The shadow of the refugee who had changed from being a pigeon whisperer and had metamorphosed into a pigeon thief. My very own shadows were beginning to scare me.

That day, I did something stupid in an attempt to fix things. I shouldn't have done it, but I was desperate. I was hoping that this would help mend things, help Yasser to leave me alone for a bit, to stop perching himself onto my shoulders like the angel of death. I was like a mountain who couldn't bear to carry any more weight. I need ed to discard this tremendous burden from my life. I was starting to have a mental breakdown. I told Yasser about the money; the one Mr. Saleh gave me. He pretended he didn't care at all. He told me that I was naive and that it wasn't about the money.

"We are doing it all for our friendship," said Yasser

"Are you being sarcastic now? What is it exactly that we are doing for each other?" I asked Yasser.

"We are here for each other." said Yasser.

I opened the gym bag and showed Yasser the birds that I had stolen from the station. He was happy and told me about his plan, but I still didn't understand what he wanted. He wanted me to train these birds; he wanted them to become carrier pigeons, delivering messages and coming back to their home base.

"Get it done, we'll meet again in a few hours," Yasser said, and then he disappeared.

***

Yasser was plotting to spy on a house, for a reason that only God, out of his ultimate wisdom, understood. I didn't know anything. He didn't tell me which house it was. I overheard him talking about it on the phone with someone. I couldn't hear where the house was located but I could tell it was near. He wanted to hook a camera to the tiny foot of a pigeon. I explained to him that if he threw the pigeon vertically like when he throws a ball, then that might give him enough time where the pigeon would be flying in the air before coming down. The weight of the camera should be enough to bring her down. I told him to bring with him a plastic bag to scare the pigeon, just in case she didn't want to fly. Sometimes they need an incentive, a trigger to fly. He tried this several times before we parted ways and it worked. I didn't ask a lot of questions. That eased the guilt I had been feeling because I was not a part of whatever he was doing and didn't know where he was going. There was a mystery to his plan. Something that he didn't want me to know. Something he didn't want anyone to know about.

To be confronted with the truth was a hard thing. Harder than the lies I kept living with, lurking in the darkness and the inner mystery of my soul. This chapter of my life was about the evil forces and the broken swords that fight a constant inner battle. This struggle was about so many things that I knew, things I didn't know and things I was going to come to know of later and live by for the rest of my life. It's hard to be stabbed in the back. Just when you think you know the truth and who your real friends are, your naivety wakes you up. Don't you feel betrayed? Don't you feel stupid and emotionally paralysed? Just when you think you know yourself. Turns out you didn't. Not at all. You feel miserable - you feel worthless.

That next morning, I saw Zara rushing out of the classroom. She looked tired and exhausted. I am sure she saw me as she passed by but pretended she didn't. She walked past me as if I was not there, as if I was a shadow. As if I was a ghost. I was concerned and I didn't know why I had a gut feeling that something bad had happened. I felt like I had done something wrong but I didn't know what. But I could feel it: the betrayal, the agony and the pain. The oh so many wrongs that I had committed. Things I couldn't redeem or forgive myself for. I kept thinking, spinning those thoughts in my head. I couldn't leave without an explanation. I wanted to know what was wrong with her. I followed her like a stalker and called her name. She didn't respond straightaway. Then I called again, and she stopped.

"Are you okay?" I asked Zara.

She told me what had happened the night before. Her words got mixed with tears and clouds. I felt that people in the street were eavesdropping on us, staring at us continuously. She told me what had happened. I started making connections about what she was telling me, vague connections in my head. I slowly connected the dots: pieces of the puzzle of what had happened the night before with Yasser and what had happened to Zara.

"What happened, are you okay?" I asked again.

"I was spied on yesterday!" As soon as she said it, she burst into tears.

I couldn't believe it. Yasser had used me to spy on Zara!

I ran back home to find Yasser. My heart was racing and I was ready to fight. I felt an urge for revenge. I was enraged. I ran to the Arab street looking for him, my feet hitting the ground loud and fast. I found him. He was sitting around a table with his friends laughing, as if nothing had happened. I stormed into the cafe and I punched him so hard that I knocked him off his chair. I was afraid he wouldn't get up. My fist was badly hurt but I was satisfied. I felt like I had wanted to do that for a long time. Seconds later I found myself being pulled outside by his gang. Ihsan walked me outside to calm me down. I was so angry and scared that I couldn't say a single word. My hand was bleeding. I was not done with Yasser yet. I didn't feel like talking to him. I didn't feel like explaining anything to Ihsan. I had never ever thought that I would punch my best friend in the face, but I did – hard - and I felt so proud.

Ihsan insisted that Yasser and I should talk. We sat in Ihsan's car. It was the last time Yasser and I interacted as friends. Our bond was broken. The world was spinning in my head with endless thoughts. Yasser felt bad for what he had done and he admitted he didn't know why he had done it. He promised to delete the footage he had. He said he didn't get any pictures and that his plan had failed. He told me that I was probably right, that certain limits are not to be crossed. Yasser asked me how he could redeem himself. I didn't want anything from him but then I thought about something – I thought I could use him for something.

"Before we part ways, I need something from you!" I told Yasser.

"Anything!" Yasser said.

"Why did you do this Yasser? Do you like Zara?" I asked.

Yasser didn't say a word. I knew he was jealous of me since the day Zara and I had been on that date. It was not about hurting me or anything. He just felt like a loser. Yasser was lonely.

"Answer me." I said.

Of course, Yasser didn't respond. I was not surprised. I trusted that with time, he would reveal his true self.

"Only time will tell Yasser. Only time will reveal who you really are" I told him.

I wanted a favour from Yasser and I knew he was going to do it for me. If he didn't do it, I would disclose everything. He knew he had no choice. That was my way of taking revenge. I didn't know how bad my plan was about to backfire.

Like a miracle, a new star was born in the Berlin pigeon sky. The man in the van was about to face a surprising fate too: the shattered glass. I saw the rock flying in the air in slow motion, hitting the glass of the van hard. Really hard. The glass collapsed before my eyes. I watched from the other side of the street, hiding behind a tree in disguise. The alarm went off and the police sirens echoed everywhere. Blue, red and white colours. Yasser jumped to the back of the van like a monkey, took the Armando pigeon and ran out from the other side. The old man was distracted, busy looking at the broken glass. I was hiding away; I was scared I might get caught too.

"Run Yasser, Run!" I shouted.

I remembered that things were not the same anymore. There was limited time to run and this was not a game. I was not sure if Yasser would cross the street or not, but the police were faster than him. Yasser ran to me, handed me the pigeon and told me to go – to disappear.

"Go Dabbour, Go!"

Not knowing what to do, I hesitated, the pigeon in my hand.

"No Yasser, don't go!"

He smiled at me and told me that it was too late.

"Take care my friend!"

I was still boiling with anger, but I didn't want my friend to go to jail. The lights from the police cars intensified and the sirens were getting so loud that I felt they were ringing in my ears. The blue, red and white lights filled my sky. Yasser had been captured. It was as if he knew this was going to happen. I didn't want this to happen, that was not my plan. I ran and ran and kept running. I realised that Yasser had surrendered himself and accepted defeat. I felt I had betrayed him and I felt bad. I was offered as a sacrifice to the wolves and the hyenas after Yasser was gone. I was the bull standing in the middle, ready to be eaten by the hungry predators, ready for them to attack me. Suddenly, I was exposed. He was a wounded horse ready to finish the race and go back to where he had come from. I went home that night and the money that Mr. Saleh had given me had disappeared.

***

I knew instantly who had taken the money. I was aware that Yasser and Ihsan had spoken about it and Ihsan had devised a way to go and steal it. To convince Ihsan to give it back would be a completely different story. To tell him I needed that money to buy birds. Good luck to me! Why did I need the birds anyway? To breed them? To stare at them? He was mocking me. He told me there could be a better use for the birds. The money, in his opinion, could be used for a better investment. The birds could be used to make even more money by smuggling drugs in the busy and sometimes abandoned train stations of Germany. Across the cloudy skies of Europe and borderless nations.

"We could make more money, buddy!" Ihsan said in a low voice.

"Ihsan, I need my money, please!"

"It's not your money, it's money that you stole from your friend the old man..."

"I didn't steal it. He gave it to me," I said.

"After you killed him and buried him in the woods?" Ihsan said.

Ihsan insisted that this money should be used to make more money. He warned me that we should stick together and if anyone of us ever got caught, we would all sink together. It was a sinking ship, our ship. But which ship? There was no ship. Nothing to hold on to. The ship had sunk in the depths of the agitated water way before it had even sailed. When you see the ship sinking, what are you supposed to do? What if you happened to be in it? Do you jump in the water or do you call for help? Do you change direction? It reminded me of the Arab world, a sinking ship that had started its painful descent many years ago, with no end in sight.

I wondered how Ihsan had snuck into our house and taken hold of the money. It must have been Yasser who had told him about it or he could even have given him a key. I was not ready for a new confrontation, but I had to fight back. I knew I was digging my own grave.

"You are digging your own grave Dabbour if you try to take the money from Ihsan." Yasser had told me a few days ago.

I wanted to feel free like a bird. I remembered I was holding the bird and lowered my gaze towards the rarest pigeon in the world, sleeping inside my jacket against the warmth of my heartbeat. At that moment I forgot everything. Memory momentarily erased. Poor pigeon didn't know what trouble was coming her way – she just joined in my misery. I was thankful for Yasser's gift. The gift that had sent him to jail.

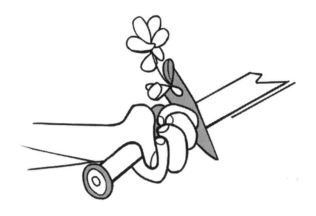

I am the sword, but I am broken. I am the good turned evil. Like gangrene corroding my soul. I am the broken sword. I am the instrument of my own demise. I am the sword: I am broken and lost. Lost, always lost, always have been.

4

THE BROKEN SWORD

I missed Mr. Saleh today and I felt that he was still here with us. I wanted to walk into his house, meet him, talk to him and tell him how much I needed him right now. I wanted to tell him how I had messed things up big time and how I wished I had listened to his advice about following the rules and trying to be a good man. To stay away from trouble. But I never listened.

I missed you, Mr. Saleh. I know that maybe I could have helped you and that under the soil in the woods, you hold within yourself bitter feelings for me and for what I have done.

To find someone who would replace Mr. Saleh was hard, almost impossible. But strangely, gradually, Ihsan started filling the void left by my old friend. He was about to become my friend: a friend I had never chosen and one I had never wanted. I was swayed like a puppet in the midst of the void, the endless limitless void.

I went to the Bellevue bridge. I wanted to immerse myself in the memories. I was dying to remember the first month I spent here in Berlin. I wanted to remember good things, like Zara, the birds and the resonating light of the setting sun in the vivid sky. I wanted to remember anything that resembled hope. I carried the Armando pigeon in my hand and watched the others fly by. I hadn't given her a name yet. I thought about returning her to her owner and leaving him a message of apology for what I had done. I guess the old man had never thought that anyone would ever steal a bird, let alone know what a rare and expensive pigeon she was.

Where was Yasser? Was he going to talk about everything we had done and every crime we had on our record? Or was he getting ready to hop on a plane and be sent back? I could picture his smile, happy to be going back. I was hoping he wouldn't mention my name. I was praying he would never do that. I found myself wishing that none of this had ever happened and that we had never been friends. Holding the pigeon in my hand, I realised Ihsan's grasp on me was similar to the control I had over that bird. He had squeezed me hard, just like I was squeezing that bird. The only difference was that his hand would crush me anytime it wanted to, anytime I overstepped my limits.

Ihsan met me after my German class and asked me about Yasser. I told him that I didn't know where Yasser was. Oblivious, I listened to the words of Ihsan. There was no one to save me at this moment, except Zara, who stood there clearly seeing how uncomfortable I was.

"Are you coming to lunch?" Zara asked me.

"Yes, just give me a second." I told Zara.

There was no lunch or anything. Zara wanted to save me from the awkward situation. Ihsan knew Zara, yet they had never talked. Ihsan would never dare talk to her. He was scared. A coward. Zara approached us and pulled me from the fangs of Ihsan. Of course, she had overheard part of the conversation.

"I told you already. I don't know where Yasser is. He didn't come home last night," I told Ihsan.

"Well, if he doesn't come tonight..." Ihsan said. He noticed that Zara could hear us and whispered. "You will have to take his place."

I walked away. He pulled me to him and whispered in my ear.

"If you know anything about whether Yasser has been captured and you are not telling me..."

Ihsan looked at me and at Zara and then at me again. He then walked away and disappeared.

Ihsan called the shots. He was desperate for something. He was escalating the pace, trying to cause as much damage as he could, keeping himself in low profile and using us in whatever way he wished. I guess he knew that if Yasser was captured then it would mean the end for him too. It would make him more vulnerable. I knew that the police were hunting us down: hunting us to the ground, hunting us to the finish line.

An unexpected encounter shifted things in a different direction. That night, Ihsan told me he was going to call me if Yasser didn't show up. He never told me what he wanted. In getting to know Ihsan, I got to know a different guy. I think he was somewhat good from the inside. But I think he was so manipulative, so good at manipulating me that he knew he needed to be sharp like a sword. The cruelty of his days had turned him into a victim. He was trying to overcome his misery. He wanted to become unbroken, but he had chosen the worst possible way. The birds were victims too.

What I hadn't noticed in the train station when we arrived was a man hiding in the dark, face unseen. I thought I was being watched and the man had followed me. I walked away from him. He was right behind me. I started running, fast. He ran faster. When he called my name, I knew who he was: it was Yasser. He was back.

How was that possible? Yasser didn't say anything. He was stiff and behaving differently. He was clearly not his old self anymore. The only words that he said were: "Let's get to work." He didn't want to talk about anything: I looked around me. Yasser acted in a calm but wary manner. I knew he was up to something.

I asked him If Ihsan knew that he was here. He replied with a yes.

"What happened to you that day?" I asked.

"What happened when?" Yasser replied.

"You tell me!" I said to Yasser.

"Dabbour, I have no idea what you're talking about!" Yasser said.

"I'm confused!" I said.

"Dabbour, stop asking questions and let's get to work!" Yasser said.

Somedays, pretending was better than just being. Pretending to be unaware of a situation was better than feeling you wanted to voice it out. Pretending to be forgetful was Yasser's coping mechanism. He was desperately trying to ease his painful sins and regrets. It was his way to forget about things; wrongs and reasons he was trying to hide from his true self. It was his way of hiding from the world. It was his way of adjusting to the confusing, contradicting world.

Ihsan didn't tell us what was coming next. We waited and waited in the empty night, hiding in the shadows until we received a message in a letter dropped to us by a random guy who passed us by. I picked up the piece of paper. It read: take Ihsan's car. Keys inside. You will find birds in the truck and a cell phone. Follow the coordinates set by the GPS and drive.

I looked at Yasser and gave him the letter to read.

"What do we do now?" I asked Yasser.

"We do what we are told, and we keep our mouths shut!" Yasser said.

"So, we've become international criminals now?" I said.

"Not literally. Just regional. European criminals."

We walked to Ihsan's car which was parked outside the train station and turned on the ignition. I picked up the phone. There was a note with GPS coordinates. I entered them into the phone.

"Amsterdam!" I said. I was shocked. "Are we about to become international criminals?" I asked Yasser.

"Soon my friend, soon!" Yasser answered.

Before we drove off, I remembered to check the trunk. There were thirty pigeons sitting there in carton boxes. The boxes were wet, and the birds were drenched in their own poop. The pigeons had tiny backpacks attached to their bodies. The tiny backpacks had small pills in them: drugs. We were supposed to take the birds to the border.

The pigeons were being used as mules to smuggle drugs, we were told. How much money was that worth, I wondered? How much money was two refugees' life worth? Nothing? Someone was smart enough to discover that the pigeons had more value than plain, simple refugees.

"Why are we doing this, Yasser? Why don't we retreat?" I asked.

"Because that's the only thing we're good at. Doing the only thing that we can do now instead of giving up!" Yasser said.

"I feel lost, Yasser!" I told him. He tried to change the subject.

"How's your little friend?" Yasser asked.

"The bird?"

"Yes!"

"I left her at home."

"That's better for her. If Ihsan learns about her, he'll chase her down and he'll want to have her like he wants everything else." Yasser said.

"Thanks for doing this, Yasser. I didn't think it would get to that!"

"I had to. I made you a promise to help you. I feel I have been failing you many times," Yasser said.

"Do you feel bad for spying on Zara?" I asked.

Yasser didn't say anything.

"The truth is..." said Yasser.

"You know what, Yasser, forget it. I don't want to talk about it. Zara and I are not together anyway. I don't want to talk about it!" I said. "Can we change the subject? It makes me feel uncomfortable."

"You are a great guy, Dabbour. Sorry for putting you through all this."

I was hoping we could try to fix things. But Yasser insisted on getting his point across.

"I could have saved you from a lot of pain. I was there when your brother screamed, and I saw him hanging by the rope. I don't know what happened to me. I froze. I didn't know what to do. I swear I couldn't move."

Yasser started crying. It was the first time I had seen him cry, ever.

"I felt jealous of you and wanted to be like you. Everyone, including myself, knew that you had a special talent. The thoughts were racing through my head at that moment. I thought I could replace your brother. I thought I could learn from you. Your brother was already falling down and hitting the ground hard. I still remember the day I remained there broken, hating myself, hating the evil nature of my thoughts..."

I really didn't know what to say. Could I even say anything at all. Why had he decided to talk about this now? I asked him. But Yasser didn't know. Maybe he thought that perhaps he could make things right and set things straight. I wondered if his intention was even an option when another crime was already in the making, sinking us deeper in our own demise.

"Can we set things straight now?" I asked.

"Maybe!" Yasser answered.

I don't know why but I felt that Yasser was hiding something from me. He had words in his mouth that he couldn't utter. Maybe it was not the right time. Maybe he was not supposed to say anything.

Life is so precious when you think you can save it. In the silence lies hope. You have hope that you can save it all. That's all you live by; the hope, only the hope that you can save your life; any life. But if you lose a life instead of saving one, how would you feel then? Maybe it was too late to feel anything at all and there was no time to even think. Reflect. Feel. The real had morphed into the unreal, into the surreal.

You see me through the window reflections of the car. You see my face and you wonder what has come by. The reflection, the image of me was all I had left. The drive was six hours long to get to the border. But there was no border. I was shocked at the scene. Something that I could never comprehend. Europe was all one big country. Where I come from was surrounded by an infinite number of checkpoints and borders. Barbed wires everywhere you went and wherever you looked.

We were asked to hand the car over to this guy who met us and take the train back. That was all that we were supposed to do. Deliver the car. In the event that we got caught, it wouldn't be Ihsan and his friends who would have been in trouble; it would have been us. The train ride was much shorter. On the way back, Yasser told me everything. He told me that he was now an informant. When he was captured by the police, he had made a deal to reveal everything about the gang. If he succeeded, he would have his visa extended, he would have a chance to stay. Maybe that was Yasser's hope of bouncing back to the right side instead of persisting on the wrong path. One thought quickly crossed my mind.

"Did you tell them about Mr. Saleh?" I asked Yasser.

"No, of course not!" Yasser said.

"What if they know? You'll be in double trouble," I said.

"They won't. That thing never happened!" Yasser said.

"You have to tell the whole truth, not half of it!" I said.

I thought that I was capable of telling the truth. I could do it. Easily. Yasser told me that he needed me to continue working with Ihsan until there was enough collected evidence. Ihsan was about to fall next and Yasser was trying to use him as a scapegoat - to save both him and me. Yasser thought his plan was going to be easy. It wasn't.

After that night, he disappeared for a few days. I wondered why. It was so sudden. That week was a week from hell. Ihsan was working with high urgency and a sense of doubt that superseded everything. Doubt was much more powerful than faith. I had the very firm belief that the game was going to be over soon. The escape game and the constant hide and seek. What I didn't know was how and when it was going to end. Nobody knew.

***

To be punished by your best friend first is awful. To have this punishment followed by one inflicted by your best friend's friend was doubly so. I was being held responsible for all of this. I was accused of betrayal and not being loyal to the gang. Far away from home, I knew things were about to get much worse. The world kept closing in on me in my tiny room like a prison cell, getting tighter and tighter every second of everyday. Zara was no longer in my line of sight. I even forget to dream about her or remember her. I realised that I had made the birds lifeless creatures, instead of keeping them by my side as the creatures of hope that they were.

"Steal more birds!" Ihsan told me on the phone.

"Steal more birds?" I said.

Was that the plan? I thought.

"All of them!" Ihsan said.

"The police will notice. We will not escape!" I said.

"That's exactly the plan," Ihsan said.

I did not understand what Ihsan wanted but I followed him all the way. Ever think of a plan that would win you time? Ihsan's idea was to gain more time. He knew he was very close to being caught. During every single night of that week, one of Ihsan's guys would drop me off at a different train station and I would leave with a bag full of pigeons. After that particular week, the whole city was aware that the birds were disappearing from the underground stations. Ihsan was plotting something else. He had a bigger plan. He wanted everyone to know he was still kicking. This put more pressure on Yasser, who couldn't execute his plan. He was also running out of time. Ihsan was like a ghost: He was everywhere and nowhere at the same time.

"So, what do you think we should do?" I told Yasser when I phoned him.

"Keep everything the same. Don't change a thing!" Yasser said.

"Yasser, I'm scared," I said, my voice vibrating through the phone line.

"Everything will be all right, my friend, don't worry!" Yasser said.

Yasser told me that we should keep a safe distance from each other until this was all over. He told me not to try to talk to anybody, not even to Anna or to Zara.

That night, I saw Anna again. Right after Yasser mentioned her. As if just thinking about the devil - made it show up right before your eyes.

"You've been busy!" Anna told me. Her words were like a punch.

She knew everything. Why didn't she arrest me?

Anna kept trying to pull my leg and I didn't say a word.

"I didn't do anything wrong! I promise."

"Please don't promise me lies."

"Why don't you arrest me if you know everything?"

Part of me wanted her to arrest me because I knew that working with Ihsan was going to be worse than being in jail.

"I thought you were a good guy, Dabbour. What happened to you? Who has done this to you?" said Anna. Her words hit me hard in the core.

"Life did. Germany has contributed to the process of corrupting my soul."

"Is it the cold weather and the cloudy sky?" Anna asked. I knew she was ridiculing me. "I want you to help yourself. Things are going to get nasty."

Anna left, leaving a lot of questions unanswered and I knew I was going to see more of her. Deep inside, she knew we were up to something. She didn't want to arrest me because that would mean losing the big prize - catching the big fish. Catching Ihsan.

Anna called me that night. For the first time, I felt that she was a woman, a real human and not just a police officer. Her call was random. The conversation was even more random. We talked about life and everything else. I felt comfortable talking to her but I didn't want to rush and make assumptions. Anna was trying to get closer to me. I thought that her femininity was a way of luring and manipulating me in order to use me.

"Believe me, I'm innocent." I told her.

"I know you are, and I want to help you!"

"I don't need help!" I said.

"Yes, you are innocent and naïve, Dabbour. You let things happen to you and you never try to take control."

"I can't!"

"I want you to steer the ship. It's your last chance!"

"I'm scared that if I do then I'll be done. Finished!"

"If you don't, you're finished. Dabbour! Open your eyes and face the truth! It's right in front of you. Staring at you in the eye!"

***

I was convinced and I was ready to move forward, trying to man up, to step up and do something right. At least one thing right. I heard some footsteps that night going up the stairs. They would fade and then I would hear them again. I opened the door of the apartment and I saw a shadow. I couldn't see the details; the image was blurred. Then I saw the face as it approached the light. I saw Yasser. His face was smashed. Beaten up. Clothes ripped apart. Cigarette burns on his arms. Yasser had beaten to death — almost.

I hurried and called a cab to the nearest emergency clinic. That call saved his life.

***

I visited Yasser later and as I walked down the hallway, I saw that Ihsan had also come to visit him. He walked past and ignored me. The big surprise was that Anna was there too, walking in after him. It was a strange encounter. Anna closed the door of the room. At first, I thought that Ihsan would leave the room arrested - in shackles. I walked a few steps closer to try to hear what they were about to say to each other. It was hard to listen.

I could hear Ihsan say, "You have nothing against me."

"You will be cornered soon," Anna said.

The conversation between them was brief and Anna walked out the door without Ihsan. How could this be? She needed solid evidence against him too. She didn't have what she needed yet. How could she prove so many things, how could she prove that Ihsan was the mastermind behind the drug smuggling? I stood outside by the door and I saw Yasser lying in bed motionless. Poor guy, he had been beaten really hard. Ihsan stood by the window, his back towards the door. I saw Yasser move his head, move an inch or two. His eyes twitching. He turned his head towards Ihsan. He was trying to tell me something. He was trying to tell me that Ihsan was the one who did it to him. We all knew it. I felt scared. Really scared. I knew that this was going to be my fate too if I dared refuse anything to Ihsan. I would be killed.

Ihsan walked out of the room and gestured for me to follow him. He didn't talk much. I could tell he was enraged. I could feel the anger in his eyes. I thought I could try reason with Ihsan, but I was afraid to get a beating too. How could you reason with a tiger when your head was in his mouth? Terrible idea.

"Ihsan, what are you doing? When is this going to end?" I said to him.

"You are coming with me!" Ihsan told me.

"Ihsan, don't be a fool. You're playing a game that you will not win. Stop. Please! Those people welcomed you. Opened their doors for you. Think about it."

Ihsan was blinded with rage. I wondered if he had been brainwashed. He had all these wrong ideas about the mechanisms of life. That life was a battle, some kind of war. He thought he was a victim being kicked in the guts and he needed to retaliate. He had the worst ideas of revenge.

"What are you trying to be, Ihsan? A drug lord in Europe? Listen, Ihsan."

I paused, taking a breath.

"I'm turning myself in!"

***

I found myself in a dark, underground room. Dust. Dust everywhere. Wires hanging from the ceiling. There was no one there. I didn't know if it was day or night. I had no means of communication with the outside world. The phone had no signal. There were pigeons in boxes; some were let loose, walking around bobbing their heads. Ihsan was sitting on a chair smoking with a computer on his lap. I scanned the place with my eyes half shut. It took me a few seconds to take it all in. Was I dead? Imprisoned? Captured? I asked Ihsan where we were. He jumped from his seat with excitement.

"I found it." he said in quiet tone.

He sat on the floor next to me and showed me his computer screen. It was a slideshow of photos. Black and white pictures. Pictures of birds. World War images. I couldn't make the connections in my head. What was he trying to tell me?

"We won't have to do anything anymore. The pigeons will do the job!" Ihsan said.

"What are you talking about? I asked Ihsan.

He closed the computer screen and put it away.

"It's called operation pigeon."

Ihsan explained to me slowly and in detail what we were going to be doing. He planned to use the pigeons to detonate bombs. How? By pecking on a target operated by the birds.

"I need you to train them, Dabbour!"

I honestly didn't know how to respond to what he was suggesting.

"I am not a criminal," I said to Ihsan.

"Are you not? You killed Mr. Saleh. I'm sure you can do this!"

I didn't ask Ihsan what we were going to be targeting. I was scared. Shivering. I even forgot to ask how on earth I had ended up here. I tried to reason with him but there was no point. Nobody could convince him.

"It's impossible. You can't win. The police is already after us!" I said.

"Dabbour, I'm not doing this for the money. Don't be stupid."

"Then why! I don't understand!" I asked Ihsan, furious?

"To send a message!" Ihsan said.

"A message of what?!" I asked.

Ihsan took a deep breath. For the first time, I felt empathy for him. I felt that he was only human.

"I cannot even explain how I have felt in those past two years, how bad I felt and how awful things were. Just because I was a stranger and I still am. I still feel that everything is my fault. It didn't matter if a German person knew me or not. They just assumed I was like any other Syrian; the reason behind the chaos and the trouble in their country. We are the perfect scapegoats. Look around you, Dabbour. It's a collective punishment to be treated like a criminal because you are labelled a refugee. I'm an engineer with a degree. Look at my life now. I've got nothing left and nothing to look forward to. I've got nothing to lose." Ihsan was overwhelmed by his emotions but somehow managed to compose himself.

"But you're not alone, Ihsan. We're all in this together!" I said, trying to make him feel better."

"Maybe we shouldn't have left Syria and let ourselves die there, buried under the rubble," Ihsan said.

"There are some refugees who made it. Right?" I said.

"Look, Dabbour. No matter what you do, you'll always be a stranger here. Understand?" Ihsan said.

"That doesn't give you the right to do what you are going to do. We have done enough," I said.

"There is no turning back. We can't go back in time now."

"There's still the option to call the police and confess everything!" I said.

Had we called the police when Mr. Saleh passed away, things could have been different. We wouldn't have had to lie all the way and we wouldn't have ended up here. Had we called the police, we would now be in a German class, learning the language of the country which had welcomed us. We would have had a job by now or even a visa allowing us to stay here lawfully.

"I'm sure there is still a way to fix this mess!" I said to Ihsan.

"It's over, Dabbour!"

"Ihsan, please. There must be a way! Please!" I said, beginning to beg.

"We're executing my plan!" Ihsan said.

"Ihsan, I have a very expensive pigeon. She's all I have left. She's worth a lot of money! Take it. Take it!" I told Ihsan.

Was I ready to give away my most precious possession? The last precious element I had. Even though it was not mine, I was holding onto it in a way that made me feel I owned it. I tried to come up with different ways to tell Ihsan to abort any potential crime he was plotting. To take a step back and put things in a different perspective.

"We all belong to the same fate," Ihsan told me. "We all belong to God and doing the right thing is the best way to redeem myself."

"I'm confused. What fate are you talking about?" I asked Ihsan.

Ihsan didn't answer. I took a second to hand him the pigeon, still living inside my jacket. She was asleep, not making a sound. Ihsan noticed the pigeon.

"What's this?"

"This is the Armando pigeon. You want money? Go sell it. You'll make a lot of money."

Ihsan held the pigeon and started rubbing his finger across her head.

"She's really pretty. Where did you get her?" Ihsan asked.

"We stole it!"

Ihsan acted surprised. I took a chance and again tried to convince him not to do anything.

"Ihsan, I can't do it. I can't do anymore harm. Please," I said to Ihsan.

"Look at your past, Dabbour. You are no angel," Ihsan said.

Every time I took a path to try to convince Ihsan to not do anything bad, he would make me feel bad about myself and lure me into victimhood. He was right. I had wasted a chance to fix everything. I had wasted so many chances. At that point, I felt that life can only give you one chance to do the right thing – only one. Either you lose it or use it.

Ihsan the drug smuggler was also a man of faith, albeit a twisted kind of faith. He believed in immorality and that was out of the question for me. He believed in revenge and violence, in taking matters into his own hands. He was doing a projection; he was trying to transfer his twisted beliefs on to me. I wondered: if we spent more time together, would we be able to transform the traumatic moments into instances of peace and tranquility? Had the world despaired with us or was it us who despised the world so much that we were constantly clashing with each other - a consistent, destructive battle?

Bits and pieces of rubble and bits and pieces of conflict and too many struggles. I wondered if we were at conflict with our own selves. Maybe that was enough to explain the state of the world we had created and the chaos we had left behind. Ihsan knew these feelings. He was acquainted with hopelessness and knew that the world was not going to get any better. So he was orchestrating his own suicide, whether that meant pulling the trigger or letting someone else do it. Even if it meant taking as many people down with him as he went down into the hellfire. The German police could do him the favour of fulfilling that prophecy for him. However he had a most fertile imagination.

If you didn't like the story in a book or the contents of a movie, you had options. Either you could turn it off and stop watching or you could close the book and stop reading. But with life, real life, how do you proceed? How do you change the course of the narrative? You had to go back in time and look carefully at your own timeline and find the moment you were born, if possible. You needed to go back in time and relive your birth, find the place and time when you came into being and trace your own history, the chapters of your life's events. You needed to try to change who and what you were, at that point in time. That metamorphosis might make a difference, but it would never change everything. It never could.

***

"I will help you!" Anna told me. I heard her voice vibrate over the phone line. "I will help you if you help me!" she said.

"How will you help me?" I asked.

"Do you want to talk over the phone"? Anna asked.

"I'll come to you. Where are you?" I asked Anna.

Anna gave me the address of her location. I was aware that if Ihsan found out I had met Anna, he would erase me. Delete me. I had to take my chances and escape furtively. I was careful to leave and come back at dawn because I knew he was going to look for me as soon as he had woken up. The door of the basement where I was stuck was open and I went in. That night, Zara sent me a message saying she had been thinking of me.

"I had a dream about you, Dabbour. I don't know if you are in Germany or not but I wanted to check if you were alright!" Zara's message read.

"What was the dream about?" I asked.

"That you were dead!" said Zara.

What did this mean? I wondered all night on my way to see Anna through the empty streets of Berlin. I played a lot of scenarios in my head: one was death. The other was life sentence in prison. Deportation was a probable option too. I had a strange feeling my end was near. I was scared that I would die and miss the birds more, especially the life spent with them. I would not be able to hold them close. I would never see them again.

In a way, I felt relieved because I felt that Zara cared about me. It didn't matter how or why but it was important that she cared, and I could feel the genuine concern. I gave all I ever had and my life to the birds. I cared for them and I didn't know how to care for any other thing or being besides them. Not even myself. My phone rang and it was Ihsan. I didn't answer at first. Then I decided to answer his call. I knew that he knew everything: where I was going and what I was intending to do.

"Don't do it!" He said.

I was so afraid to die. I was scared. I was so close to the cafe where Anna was waiting for me. I decided to retreat.

I called Anna.

I'm sorry, Anna. I'm really sorry." Then I hung up.

***

I was stuck in the middle. Torn between Ihsan and Anna. Pulled in every direction. I felt so scared for my life. Scared like never before.

I joined forces with the devil, and I knew there was a maximum number of errors that life could tolerate from you and forgive you for. After you reached that threshold, life could not tolerate you anymore.

Tonight, Zara and I would meet in my dreams. The good dreams. Tonight, we would live up to the highest creeds: the purified one, free from sins and bad fate. The set of beliefs that I had failed to live by and failed to follow, like a path with land mines and danger signs.

"I'm guilty and I'm ashamed," I told Zara.

And I cried like a child, fell into her arms like a lost lover weeping all night.

"I know you are innocent. You better leave it all behind and start anew," Zara said.

"What are you talking about?" I asked her.

"The police knows everything. You have to prove it - turn yourself in." Zara said.

"If I turn myself in..." I said.

"It's the only choice you have. Everything you have ever dreamt of will vanish if you don't. Do it. For love. For the last hope you've got," Zara said.

"What if your dream comes true?" I asked.

"Go, Dabbour. Go. Turn yourself in. Everything will be over soon," Zara said.

On that note, the night fell. The darkness set into the last stage of a deeper shade - darkness that knew no daylight and no tomorrow. The day felt distant, like a million light years away, like a distant star out of reach, out of touch with life. An ephemeral star that had not been allowed to shine its brightest.

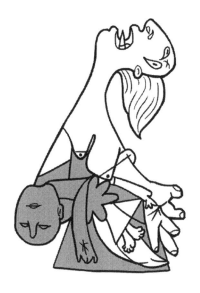

I am the law and the rules. I am the force of governance. I am the tough one. I make sure that justice always prevails. My eyes are always wide awake, and I live with worry and concern every single day. I make sure that good and justice prevails with my existence in the world.

5

THE OPEN-MOUTHED WOMAN

I wanted to depict the map of my life for Anna. I felt the urge to explain things but every time I tried, the words would get stuck in my throat, as if on mute. I was unsure whether she would understand or if my story would even mean anything to her, the whole story – my story. We were two people speaking two different languages. We were lost, the words were lost. So lost that we would probably need an interpreter to make sense of the unclear meanings, even when just uttered. Sometimes they would get interrupted by mere silence falling in between spoken words.

"Stop Dabbour," she said.

I told her that I had nothing to tell her at this point and she asked me why I was still insisting on doing the wrong thing. She could not understand why I was persisting on that path. I didn't know what to say: I never really knew what to say. I had no answers left.

"Aren't you tired of the chasing and running away?" said Anna as she parked the car and stepped out. She was tall and I felt I was going to strain my neck just by looking up at her.

"I genuinely don't have anything to tell you. I just want peace. I want to be left alone!" I said to Anna.

"How can you have peace when you are at war with yourself?"

I told her that I was scared. That I was scared of everything.

"What are you scared of?" Anna asked.

"I'm afraid to face the same fate as Yasser'!" I said.

"I can help you!"

I was really fed up with this self-pity. I was ready to walk away and leave it all behind. I told Anna that I didn't need any help. She then told me that I had changed. That's when I remembered that she was living in a different world, in a comfortable bubble from where she could not understand where I was coming from and the journey which had brought me here to Germany.

"What did you think, that I'd still be the same after all this, really?"

"How can I help you?" Anna asked.

"Send me back!"

I told Anna that I wanted to be sent back home. I confessed to her that I wanted this whole phase to be over and for this living nightmare to end. I was opening up to her, hoping that my voice would reach the very depths of her soul.

"Do you think it's that simple? There's a process for that!"

"Screw the process!" I said. I was ready to break all the rules.

Anna was aware that, after Yasser, I was the only lead they had to arrest Ihsan. She insisted and I resisted. She told me to hit the record button on a tiny recording device she was holding in her hand.

"When you meet Ihsan, just hide it in your jacket and press record. Then, everything will be over." Anna said.

I took the device and walked away, not knowing why I was even doing it. I went to meet Ihsan, knowing deep inside that I was dragging myself towards my own demise.

***

Upon meeting Ihsan in the Arab street, we sat on the side of the road and talked. And talked. I was waiting for him to share his plans with me but he didn't reveal anything. Deep inside, he knew that he was going to get caught sooner or later and he felt the world closing down on him. He became cautious. It was just a matter of time before it was all over. Everything was going to end soon. I knew it. Ihsan loved to show how strong and how fearless he was: but that was all nonsense. He was camouflaging his own fear. He was scared too. I had to get him to talk. I had to find out what his plan was but Ihsan just would not talk. He just wouldn't. He got suspicious. He was careful, really careful this time.

"What's the plan tonight, Ihsan?" I asked.

"The plan is that you turn yourself in." Ihsan said.

I was in shock and I stuttered. I shivered.

"What do you mean?" I stammered.

"Give yourself in Dabbour. Redeem yourself!" Ihsan said. "Dabbour, you are the best thing that has ever happened to me. You are my best friend." said Ihsan. I realised that he was drunk, so intoxicated that he didn't even know what he was saying. He was swaying as he uttered these words. What a glaringly contradictory image of faith and drunkenness. A display of holy ignorance mixed with the pathetic nature of human beings unfolding right in front of my eyes.

Ihsan had planned and plotted to make me the villain of the story, the villain of Germany. As if I wasn't already, as if I hadn't made mistakes in the past and committed crimes and sinned. Was it regret for everything that he had done that drove him to this madness? Ihsan was guilty and he didn't want to pay the price for all his wrongdoings. He was scared to face the reality of his faults. He wanted someone else to pay for his mistakes: and he had chosen me. He wanted someone to bear the weight of all his sins, his crimes and the pain he had suffered throughout his life. Ihsan had always felt that he was the victim and it was time for him to project that feeling onto someone else. He was in denial, in absolute denial. And so was I. He failed to face reality or do the right thing. He was blind, mad and bad. He had learnt to carry the weight of the world on his shoulders. What burdened him: the war, the migration problem, the Syrian refugees, the rebels, the bombs and the gun shots. Everything was crushing him down, like a heavy rock on his shoulders. He couldn't carry it anymore, it had become unbearable.

I felt like I was ageing too while listening to Ihsan's last words, slow and heavy. The words faded out like the sounds of trains fading away in the distance, like the unstoppable force of the screeching brakes on the rails, like the relentless force of time, like the first day the story had started. It rained that day and the rain was heavy and hard. It was dark and muddy. Just like my life.

"You're going to confess Dabbour!" Ihsan said.

"Confess? To what?" I asked.

"Confess to the world and tell them what you did!" Ihsan said.

"I didn't do anything!" I said, knowing it was already too late. I had said this, knowing I had come to this realisation after the curtains had been drawn.

"Dabbour my friend, admit it. You're the master-mind behind it all. Did you forget?" Ihsan said. He was so serious that I almost believed him and submitted to his wishful thinking. Everyone was gone. All my friends. And here I was all alone, struggling to understand the bewilderedness I was finding myself in.

"But I'm innocent!" I said living by the hope that this would change something, anything.

"Someone has to pay the price for our sins! Take a look at the world Dabbour. Who's paying the price for the chaos and the misery? Take a closer look my friend!" Ihsan said.

"We are!" I said affirming Ihsan's ideas.

"Exactly, do you know why?" Ihsan asked me.

"Because we are the weak ones. The weak always pay the price!"

Deep inside, Ihsan knew that I would surrender and that I would not dare run away. Life. Oh, why have you done this to me? What did I do to deserve this? Oh life, grant me a different narrative and a different ending - maybe a house by the ocean, a beautiful warm house with a nice cosy bed to lie down and dream at night. I wanted to grow old. I wanted to love and live a normal life. Was it supposed to be that hard? Was it only a dream? Was I asking for too much? I would love to be given a second chance, a different take on life. I prayed and prayed that God would offer me something else. I prayed that the universe would answer my call and my supplications.

I walked back into the Berlin apartment. The night was pitch black dark and I started remembering the day I had arrived in Germany two years ago. I had become afraid of the unknown and scared of the worst possible scenario: going back home. If only I knew what home was. I also felt that this new place was like a home to me – I felt free and I felt a sense of justice and fairness I hadn't experienced before. I was torn between the two burning flames in my heart: the East and the West: One world didn't want me and the other had trouble welcoming me.

When I met Anna again, she was waiting for me to hand her the tape recording. She was hoping there would be something on it. But when she played it, there was only noise. Air. Wind. She looked at me and her face was blank. It scared me. I was still shivering from the cold freezing air outside, still not accustomed to the warmth of her car.

"You failed again Dabbour!" said Anna.

"I want to tell you that I'm innocent." I said.

"That should have been your confession!" said Anna.

I wanted a guarantee from Anna that if I did tell her everything, I would get something in return. Something. Anything to hold onto. But she couldn't guarantee me anything. She was lost and confused. Stuck in an endless cycle, of thoughts, just like me. We didn't have time. We were fighting time. Time was not on our side.

"I'm ready to speak!" I said to Anna.

Anna took the recorder from me and held it in her hand. She then pressed the record button.

"Are you ready?" asked Anna.

"Where do I start?" I asked.

"Start from the beginning…" said Anna.

I paused. I hesitated. I knew I wouldn't. I knew I couldn't. Anna sighed. We both looked out the window, contemplating the misery the outside world was capable of inflicting on us. I thought about what had happened to Yasser. To be dead in your own land or a prisoner in a foreign land. Which one was worse? Both were unfortunate fates but if only you had the freedom to make your own choices. Maybe it was meant to be that I would have to take matters into my own hands and end this story once and for all, but how? My mind was racing and my heart was beating fast. I walked back to my apartment and Ihsan hugged me when he saw me.

"So, are you ready to go?" Ihsan asked me.

"Why did you choose me?" I asked.

"Because you are the most innocent one Dabbour." Ihsan said. "It's the only way the whole story will make sense."

"How can you have a good conscience and just free yourself from all the responsibility?" I asked.

Ihsan didn't say anything.

"What if I don't want to confess?" I asked.

"It is too late my friend..." Ihsan said.

Someone had to pay the price. I had been chosen.

***

When your life is sacrificed, when you are offered as the ultimate sacrifice. How many deaths can your soul take? I was about to be forced into believing that the biggest sacrifice was the most beloved one of all. I had to commit to sacrificing my most beloved companions, the birds.

"Steal the birds, steal them from all the train stations." Ihsan said to me on the day that was going to be the final chapter of my story. I didn't know how this was going to end. I didn't know how it had all begun. I had no route of escape, in fact, I had no route at all. I was stuck. Physically and mentally. That night, we counted all the birds we had collected; there were 500 or more. They were stacked in gym bags without food or water; had I become their slayer instead of their keeper? I wondered.

"Can we at least give them food?" I asked Ihsan.

They were only going to make it for a short while, several hours maybe, if they remained where they were. We were on the run. I was forced to remember the scene vividly all my life, standing in the midst of the outdoor market on a Sunday morning. I didn't know what Ihsan wanted from me or when we were going to release the birds. Nor did I know where he intended to do it. He whispered in my ears – my body was shaking and all my senses went numb.

"This is it; this is Operation Pigeon." Ihsan said.

How could Ihsan even think that I was going to partake in such a heinous act; but he knew how to manipulate me. I asked him what our target was, but he wouldn't answer. Finally, he did and pointed to the sky. I wasn't sure why.

"Wait for it" Ihsan said. "It's going to be a pleasant surprise."

"A pleasant surprise?" My laughter was loaded with pain.

Could there be any more pleasant surprises left? How bad could things get, just how bad?

It was a trap. I was the scapegoat. I was Ihsan's escape. He was smart. From the beginning, he had thoroughly studied me and had come to understand my thinking processes; how I perceived things and my potential reactions. Ihsan had lead me to believe that the birds were carrying bombs and detonators. He had tricked me into believing all sorts of false things. All my thoughts were preoccupied with the certainty that I was meant to get confused. But it was too late for confusion; I knew that my actions would lead me to jail, forever. Ihsan had calculated my steps, ten minutes before the operation was meant to happen. The zero-minute approached. We sat in his car, parked on the side of the road. He knew I was thinking of running away. I was bleeding from inside and didn't know what to say to him or to my desperate self.

"Thank you, Dabbour!" Ihsan said.

"Why Ihsan? Why are you doing this to me?" I asked.

"Because you are a gift – a gift from the sky to me," said Ihsan.

"A gift? What are you talking about?" I said.

A gift that he kept using to further his own and his friends' interests. A gift from the sky? The birds were the ones meant to be gifts but we were turning them into rocks falling from the sky over our heads and car windows.

"Thank you! I wish you luck my friend." said Ihsan.

He stepped out of the car and locked me up inside. There was no way out for me. I banged my fists and my head on the glass like a bull. German cars were sturdy like solid blocks of steel. I saw Ihsan talking to the police. He made sure I knew he was calling them and that they were on their way. He stood closer to the window. I kicked and kicked, desperately trying to open the door, but it was locked and there was no way out. He pushed his face into the glass. He was so close that I could see his breath fogging up.

"The birds are carrying drugs in their tiny bag packs." Ihsan said.

I understood.

I managed to crawl into the backseat and through the opening into the trunk. I kicked and kicked, and eventually it opened. There, I saw the birds wearing their tiny backpacks. I was blinded. Everything was blurred and all I could picture was the police coming to get me. I knew the end was coming my way. I had to sacrifice the only thing left, the birds. I had to release them all and there was not enough time to do it. There were electric wires high over my head and I had to think fast. The only way out was to let the birds go—all of them. Five hundred birds went flying into the electric wires causing a massive fire. They were instantly turned into ash. Fortunately, this street was quite deserted at that time. The birds were instantaneously burnt into chunks, their stench overwhelmed me. It was a collective punishment. I knew it was a losing game, to lose both the innocent birds and the drugs they were carrying. There was a huge fireball in the sky and my heart was sore from the feeling of betrayal felt by the pigeons towards me as their gracious bodies turned into flames.

My phone rang. It was Ihsan again.

"What did you do Dabbour? Are you crazy? Ihsan said, screaming.

"I did what I had to do." I said.

Then I realised it was a game.

"There were no bombs, right?" I asked.

"No." Ihsan said.

"Drugs?" I asked.

"No, you were project pigeon. Thank you, my friend."

I knew that Ihsan hadn't called the police either, his plan had worked. He had caught me on video creating this massive fire. The video was now all over the internet. Everyone had seen it. The whole world.

"Why did you do this?" I asked.

"It was about time you confessed to everything you have done Dabbour – no more hiding and no more running away. If you confess, maybe you can save yourself a lifetime in prison…" said Ihsan.

He wanted someone to bear the weight of all his sins, his crimes and the pain he had suffered throughout his life. He had always identified himself as the victim. He had failed to grasp the true reality of his despicable actions. He was blinded. And mentally affected. The war, the migration problem, the Syrian refugees, the rebels, the bombs and the gun shots. It had all taken a huge toll on his psyche.

The tragic end of the birds paralleled my own ending. Now the police were on their way for real and I had a few minutes or maybe seconds of silence and peace to close my eyes and reflect on everything. What do I do now? What do I do before the storm, while the fire was still raging outside. I crawled back inside the car from the trunk and jumped into the driver's seat. I grabbed my phone and I turned on the video and started recording. It was time to tell the world who I am, what I was and what I had done.

And this is how the whole night unfolded in its mysterious beauty. I sat by the window of the car looking at the raging fire. I waited for the world to have its final say and call its people and citizens to sanction my action. I sat there in the car; fire mixed in the shade of the blue light coming from outside. Ihsan was gone. The video was all over the web and I was trapped inside a spider's web. I was so lonely and unforgiving of everything. I sat there, as if glued to the car seat. Who would have known that the last seconds of being in Germany would have been spent in such a dramatic way? Who would have thought that Dabbour the innocent introvert only had a few minutes left before everything would come to an end? The phone rang and my heart beat out of fear. It was Zara.

"Dabbour, I saw the video..."

Zara was crying. I could hear her weeping from afar. I could even picture her in her apartment, tears dripping down her eyes on to the floor and on to her bed.

"I'm sorry I made you cry," I said.

I felt strange about my reaction.

"You, Dabbour? I can't believe it!"

"I'm sorry, Zara."

"Why, Dabbour, why?" Zara asked me.

"There was no other way. Believe me!" I said.

"Please tell me that you are innocent," Zara said.

"I'm not, Zara. I'm not."

Did Zara thought I had a choice? Had I been given the permission to feel, by my own self, I would have expressed what it meant to love – because I loved her for sure. To be certain of love and to be certain of the truth. The truth that comes from the anticipation of giving all the love you have on the inside. The pages were turning, times were changing, and the clock was ticking, fading away like the rays of the sun on the last day on earth. How did I transition from feeling somewhat safe in my little apartment to being left alone to an unknown fate? Where do I go from here now? Lost in the moment, a quick flash of thought connected the space and the distance between Damascus and Berlin. The sirens arrived from the distance and the video was now in the hands of the world - it had travelled faster than the speed of light.

In the end, if you find yourself on the good side of things, you were lucky. Your book would be handed to you in your right hand. If your bad deeds outweighed the good ones in the ultimate balance of rewards, you would have your book handed to you in the left hand. The video was playing in loops in my head and I heard my voice a million times coming from every corner of the apartment. It seemed to me like every apartment in Berlin, every single house was watching the footage at the same time. My face would be memorised and eventually recognised by everyone. There was no way to hide anymore. This was me. This was Dabbour, the Pigeon Whisperer.

"Someone had to speak the truth," I told Zara.

"Someone? Dabbour, did you do it?" she asked.

"There is no way to go back now," I said, my voice fading. "I hear the sirens. I have to go..."

I hung up. Zara knew something. Perhaps something that I didn't know. Something about me that maybe I myself didn't even know. That I was innocent maybe? If only I knew. After everything I had done, did I still have my own doubts about myself? I didn't know. I never really knew who I was. I had to live to this moment to tell the world who I was and the crimes I had partaken in; the killing of Mr. Saleh, the drug smuggling and everything else.

Now that I was able to think about it all, I wish I had another chance. I wish that the fear would go away. Sometimes in life, we think we have time to do everything we plan and we delay. And we wait. We continue to wait. We wait to believe that tomorrow we will live. Tomorrow we will hope to live again. Tomorrow we will fall in love. Tomorrow we will laugh. Tomorrow we will smile. What if tomorrow never comes and we don't wake up? Then we would have wasted our chance to live and think of all the things we had always wanted to think of, but it might already be too late. I felt sad. But somehow this sadness was liberating. That finally this was all over and that I would be going back to Syria soon. Now I would go back and accept the fact that war was ravaging my country, hoping that one day the misery would end. I had tried, by coming to Germany, to change the world I lived in, but the world did not want to change at all. Maybe it would have been better if I had never left at all.

The video continued playing and the number of online views was going up by the minute. The video was on loop, endless loop in everyone's lap and on everyone's device. I heard my voice ache as a I tried to speak up, I choked as I held the phone in my hand and started recording my final confession to the world:

I am Dabbour. I am the Pigeon Whisperer and this is my story: I'm a drug smuggler and a murderer. My life has and always will revolve around my birds. I loved them and still do. When I first came to Germany, I thought I would find heaven, the life I was looking for. I thought that it would be easy to learn the language and get along with everyone, but it was not easy. I had fled from the warplanes and the oppressive political system. I came here with my friend Yasser. It was here that I fell in love for the first time (Zara, I still love you. Yes, I do) and my heart beats at the very remembrance of you. You are the perfect girl who befriended a simple someone like me - a pigeon whisperer. You broke my heart, and I had to find real friends. I found birds wandering around train stations and thought about using them to smuggle drugs in order to make more money. I got better each time. One day I met Mr. Saleh, an owner of a pizzeria. Mr. Saleh was also Syrian; he liked me and knew about my love for the birds and offered me a deal to turn this into a business. Because I was greedy, I decided to kill Mr.

Saleh and I buried him in the woods. Mr. Saleh, I'm sorry. I stopped everyone who tried to get in my way. I knew I had done so much wrong, a lot of bad things but I felt good about myself for the first time in my life. I beat my friend Yasser when he tried to stop me. I almost killed him. Yasser, I'm sorry. Every time I engaged in a bad deed, the pain was excruciatingly numbing until I could no longer feel anything. I had become fearless. It's me, Dabbour. I am the pigeon whisperer. I am all these things. A friend of mine once told me: follow the rules if you want to stay in Germany. I never listened. I wish I did.

End of video.

I wish I had listened.

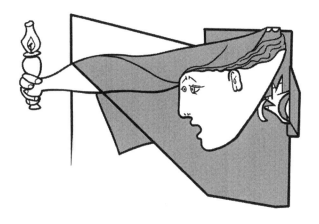

I am the woman with the oil lamp. I am the drop of oil in the lamp, sitting still in the dark. I am the last bit of hope. I am love and I am the light. I am the shoulder you cry on at the end. I am your flame, I am your love – your endless love. I am your destiny.

6
THE WOMAN WITH THE OIL LAMP

It does feel painful when you have to write your own chapter with your own ink and write your words with your own blood. It makes you feel scared that the night will smear the pages and ruin the words written on them.

I ran back to the apartment to find a place to hide. Feet hitting the ground hard. I waited for the call. The call I had waited for all my life. The call that came at the wrong time – a bit too late. The voice I heard and the curtains that swayed. Behind them I hid like a criminal, behind them I hid like a ghost. I reflected on the concepts of wrongdoing and good doing and the space in between them. I thought about a world fading away like a mirage. I thought about everything, but the call interrupted it all. It was Zara's voice again. Sometimes all you need is a tiny ray of hope, like the drops of oil in a lantern, like hazy light on a dark night. Sometimes that's all you needed to feel alive again. I listened carefully to what Zara said. I could hear the sirens echoing everywhere. How could I go anywhere when her voice was everything? I needed to feel zen.

"Hang in there. I'm on my way to you!" Zara said.

I told her not to come. It was all going to be over soon.

Zara didn't listen. She remained on the line.

"Don't hang up on me! Zara said.

I lost track of time; the minutes passed in between my heavy breathing and the soaring engine of the cars. Soon enough I was barraged by the police, men and women running in their uniforms up the stairs. I had hoped that Zara would arrive before the police so that I could see her before being taken away. Everything was over and done with fast. It was all over – in the blink of an eye.

Let me tell you about the next part of my life and the twist of fate which occurred. Many times I have felt as if I was never alone. I had failed to see a lot of things. I was in the midst of all these shades and colours. I felt like a witness standing in the middle surrounded by all these people I knew and all those who had passed by me. I looked at each one; those who had failed to know me like I had failed to know them. I wanted freedom and I felt like I had banged my head against the walls like a bull many times over and over again.

The trial felt like the last day on Earth. Eyes staring at me amongst the corridors and from inside the courtroom like snakes crawling over my back ready to attack with their poison. The whole vibe was poison. I felt weak, so fragile and ready to be compromised, already compromised.

A few months went by and in the tiny prison cell, I saw a shadow of a visitor walking through the jail cell door at night. At first, I thought he was the angel of death or maybe the angel of salvation. I thought I had seen a ghost – a good ghost I had dreamt of into my own reality.

Mr. Saleh's face was glowing in the dark. I heard his voice echo in the jail cell walls.

"I had hoped that you would listen to my advice. You could have saved yourself a lot of trouble," Mr. Saleh said.

Mr. Saleh's image started to fade away as he walked away from me.

"Please, don't leave me hanging in here like this," I begged.

Mr. Saleh slowly walked back to me and put his arms around my shoulders.

"Son, all I wanted was to be given a proper funeral. After all these years living in the diaspora, the least I had hoped for was a decent funeral."

Mr. Saleh disappeared.

A week later began a three-year trial period.

***

To be given love that you have wished for is a miracle. It felt like a blessing you feel you don't deserve. I thought I was going to stand alone in front of the judge and in front of the world. I was guilty, after all, wasn't I? I deserved any destiny that was chosen for me. I wasn't aware that I could ask for a lawyer to defend me against everything I had done. But even so, I couldn't afford it.

One day in the courtroom, Zara showed up without prior notice. She was there, as perfect as ever, standing up for me, representing me as my lawyer.

"Why are you doing this?" I asked Zara.

"You don't deserve to go to jail, Dabbour," Zara said to me.

"I don't deserve what you are doing for me either, Zara," I said to her as we stood outside the courtroom.

"I'm doing this because it's the right thing to do."

The right things that had gone wrong. I knew I needed a miracle to fix it all up. I knew I needed a miracle to bring things back to normal or as normal as they could ever be.

I relived it all in my mind. The pigeons dropping dead from the sky. The birds losing their friend at the Bellevue bridge. I still had a taste of the woods in my mouth from the day I had buried Mr. Saleh. I could still hear the screeching sound of the metal from the day he had saved me. I still remember the tears the day Zara told me she didn't love me.

Slowly, things were about to unfold like the foam floating to the surface of the ocean revealing itself. Zara came to the trial and never missed a day. It made me love her secretly even more. Watching her perform. Watching her give me her everything. Watching her sacrifice it all, just for me. I was secretly falling in love with her even more. I could feel the doors of Heaven opening up again. It was like the trial of the day of judgement where you will find yourself completely naked, ready to be recompensed for your deeds. And you can't help smiling. Deep inside, you are scared but something soothes your being as you are slowly washed clean of all your sins. Your past is ripped away from you and everything that constitutes who you are: there you stand all alone facing destiny, facing eternity.

Zara knew that she could win. She tried to convince the judge that I could leave prison on bail until my trial was over. The judge agreed. Zara knew that there was no real evidence to detain me. She and everyone else knew that Ihsan was the real mastermind behind it all. There were certain times I could leave the house and a set route I could walk along. I accepted the offer; I had no other option. I took it. I was happy.

"When will this all end?" I asked Zara as we were riding in her car back home.

"It'll all be over soon. I promise you," Zara said.

"You are taking a risk, Zara; you didn't have to do this!" I said.

She didn't say anything. She stopped the car in front of my old apartment. With a kiss on the cheek, she left. I couldn't sleep that night, I kept tossing and turning in my bed. I wanted to leave the apartment and get some fresh air. I managed to sneak out at night hoping that no one would see me. I went to the Bellevue bridge. I wanted to be there and stay all night. I went there and there were no birds. It seemed as if the pigeons had migrated to a different land. I waited and waited for them, but they never came. It reminded me of Mr. Saleh's rooftop where birds used to visit sometimes, as if to have a date with us. I walked back home, and, on the way, I stopped by the train station. There were no trains. It was late, past midnight. I sat by a bench and waited for the next train, which meant it was a couple of hours of more waiting. Looking around that station, I immediately recognised it: it was the same underground station where everything had started. I thought I was going to see Yasser, but I didn't. Then I saw a bird walking in the distance, near the tracks. It was slowly approaching me and I thought that maybe she recognised me. And I recognised her too. It seemed to me that we had met before somewhere in a different life.

***

I saw it all, the trial. My trial and the things unfolding in the void. Unfolding in front of my eyes. I saw it, the trial of life and the life we had been promised. But life was no longer delivering its promises. The trial in the German courts was lasting forever. Back and forth every day. The never-ending sessions, the voices of the judge, the witnesses. My own and my lawyer's, Zara. Where do we go now, and where do we roam? The endless times and the lifeless times in the waiting rooms, tiny prison cells and the court room. There I was again, standing in the gloom of the room. I witnessed the fierceness with which Zara defended me – somehow her determination revealed a glimpse of the true me. I was tired and could not wait for this to end, but there was no end – there was no light at the end of the tunnel. There was no view of any kind of end in sight. Vision was completely blurred.

One day before the trial was due to start, I felt Zara's hands on my shoulder. Her voice was soothing like music. Her hands landed on my shoulder like a gracious butterfly. She told me that it was very likely that I would be getting out of jail on bail. I had so many questions about her motivations for helping me. I didn't deserve any of it. I felt like a loser. I felt I didn't deserve any help.

"What do we do now?" I asked Zara when she drove me home.

"We wait." She said.

"For how long? I feel like we're back to square one." I said.

"Are you tired of waiting?" Zara asked.

"I am tired of living a pseudo life." I said.

"You don't have to wait anymore. It's all over." said Zara.

"What do you mean?" I asked her. My heart beating fast.

"They dug up Mr. Saleh's body. Autopsy shows he died of a heart attack." Zara said.

"That means…" I uttered.

"You are innocent. You are free." Zara's words were everything I wanted to hear.

I closed my eyes and took a deep breath.

***

That was the day I packed my bags and was ready to go. That was that day I recalled everything very vividly. The last time Zara and I saw each other in my Berlin apartment. I felt my heart warm like a lantern's light. I felt warmth on the inside. Winter was gone and Zara and I had met in an ice-cream parlour. I chose mint and she opted for chocolate.

"So that's it? You're going?" asked Zara.

I smiled. I didn't have anything to say to that. "Yes."

"Why do you want to go? Where do you want to go?"

I wanted to explain everything to her: that there was nothing like home – but what is home? My foggy brain was still slowly clearing up like the sky rids itself of thick clouds after winter. I felt my body going through these processes; I was longing for spring, the blooming flowers and the calm. Was it the same back there? Was it peaceful? Was it the peace you felt? Was it the remedy you felt after losing it all? Was it the repetitive melody of the bombs, the guns and the war? Was it the same back home? Were flowers the same? And the songs and the lovers? What was home like? A sky clogged with firefighters and agony? I wondered if our orange sky was painted with pigeon wings and flocks of birds or had it been painted over by the yellow poison of gas and the toxic colour of war. I wanted to tell it but then I was taken aback by Zara's voice again and her question.

"Are you going where the war is over?" Zara asked.

"I don't know!" I said.

Zara felt her heart ache and I could see the pain reflecting in the shimmer of her eyes.

"Your ice-cream has melted. You forgot to eat it." I said.

"Yours has melted too." said Zara.

There was a special connection between us, unspoken words and feelings that I couldn't escape — was it happy or sad? Pure or contaminated? This newborn bond felt like the ultimate cure. It was like love but not love. It was like light and hope. Timid, shy hope. The kind of hope that you learn to trust, after all the misery your life had subjected you to. The kind of hope that makes you picture a plane in the sky — a firefighter — metamorphose into a paper kite. The kind of hope that makes you believe that the worst raging fire in the sky can be turned into cool water. The kind of hope that encourages you to trust that life will put on your path people who will genuinely love you, even after your most loyal friends have deserted you. Hope that lifts you up and extracts you from the darkness and forces you to see the light of the new day, again.

I knew that there was a tremendous amount of energy that could come from a single personal sacrifice. I was not a convict anymore. I was not being chased anymore. I was not running around chasing dust with illusions chasing me.

"You can still make your dreams come true. Find a job. Get a visa. Live it up." Zara said.

I was not ready to go back and start over again. I was not.

"And you can still live your dream of owning the birds again."

"Zara, you don't understand. I still feel guilt." I said.

The scar of guilt was not going to leave, how could it ever?

"You need to forgive yourself."

How do I forgive myself? For burdening the birds with a despicable sin. How do I draw the image of the free spirit in my head. How do I become the captain of my life again? How do I depict the image of a burden-free love? A few hours before I was due to travel, I was looking for the old man with the van. I wanted to return his fancy bird, the Armando, but I couldn't find him. He was not there. I owed him an apology for taking his animal and for the broken glass, but he was not there. I held the precious bird in my hand, gazed towards the sky and set her free to where she belonged. Simultaneously, I set my soul free. She was the gift that I had never deserved and which I had never earned. I was the bird I never wanted to be, the traveler who had never found home. With the Armando pigeon leaving my hands towards the wide-open sky – I was ready to say goodbye to all the birds in my life and start anew. Painful? Yes. But it was all going to be alright, wasn't it?

Germany had offered me the chance to extend my visa to stay if I accepted to use my talent to help them take care of wandering birds in the train stations. I refused the community service and said no. I said no to it all. I felt bad for Yasser and all the others. I didn't even know what had ultimately happened to them. Was Ihsan caught after everything he had done? What about Yasser and the promises to allow him to stay in the country? Did he want to stay, or had he already left? We had all ended up going our separate ways and we were destined to never meet again.

The hardest goodbye was the one exchanged with Zara. It was hard for her. It was hard for me. But I was ready to move on.

"How do I thank you for everything you have done?" I asked Zara when she dropped me at the main station.

"Do you always thank people by telling them goodbye?"

When words fail you, silence was the best option.

"I can't stay Zara. I have made up my mind." I said.

Then there was silence. Again.

Then I spoke to her in Arabic. Words that were purposely never meant to be understood and that I never translated for her. Zara never understood what I had told her. Her eyes widened as I uttered those words. Her eyes welled up as if she understood what my heart was trying to tell her.

"Who's the stupid girl who loves a pigeon whisperer?"

We went our separate ways.

***

In the main central station, the scene was different but still felt the same. I was lucky to be here, to be blessed with the mercy of God and the acceptance of the world. It could have been worse, a lot worse. To be free meant to never be complete; it was bitter like the taste of Turkish coffee in my mouth. For the first time, I felt ready to stop the race against my own self. I felt at peace but as I boarded the train and stood at the gate hearing the final announcement, I was facing the unknown.

"I know why you go to German classes."

It was the voice of the past calling me, slicing through the ultimate decision-making moment. Memories flooded in between the picture standing before me and Yasser's voice.

He knew why I went to the German classes; he knew and once again, after all this time, as is characteristic of my old friend, he showed up from nowhere to tell me to rethink my plans. Think of the times you walked in the streets alone, think of the times we took decisions together, drank tea, screamed at each other. Think of what you loved and what you love now: for once, think about yourself. Put yourself first.

"Yasser?"

"Why did you let her go?"

"How did you know?"

"It doesn't matter. If after everything you have done, you are going to give up now, then you must be a fool."

I had to admit that Yasser's voice had resonated with the voice of reason within myself. I was unsure of what I was doing; I could not differentiate between real and fake. I had to find the way home, again. There was a grey thin line between giving up and taking one more step forward. I took a step closer towards the soft wind blowing, from the approaching train.

I took a step, about to board.

"Don't let her go, Dabbour." Yasser's voice echoed again.

"I can't change anything now. It's all done."

"Nothing is done unless you think it's done." Yasser's voice faded out.

It was all quiet now. The train had stopped. Yasser's voice was now muted. I looked behind me and he was gone. I could only listen to my own inner voice and my heavy breathing. I had seconds to decide what to choose. Should I go back home and try to make this place my home again? It didn't really matter who I was anymore so why did I care about the stigma? Why worry about being called an outcast, a liar, a pigeon thief? None of that really mattered. I felt for the first time that I was happy to be burden free. I was still what I was and what I would always be. I took a step back and stepped down the train. As I was doing so, a pigeon landed next to my feet. When you have the choice to follow your heart or follow the path designed by life's grand design, which one do you choose? I followed my heart. The voice telling me to go back and be with Zara was powerful. Very powerful. I took a deep breath and walked out of the train station, hoping her car would still be there. What about Syria? A part of me will always be attached to my roots, my school, the old souq, the rooftop, the house, my birds, my family, my language and my faith. I will have Syria in me. Forever. I didn't hold all the keys to the truth, but I knew at this point that home would always live inside me and that I would carry it with me like my mother carried me in her belly. Syria was my mother. We share a bond like no other. One day, maybe very soon, I would go back to Syria and I would live at home. I would knock on its door and it would welcome me, as if I had never left. I would immerse myself into its homely beauty; I would breathe its air and its air would breathe me.

Interview with the Author
by Journalist Sherouk Zakaria

S: First of all, tell us who is Motaz H Matar?

M: I am Motaz H Matar, an Arab, a Palestinian born in Amman, Jordan. I have lived most of my life in the city of Amman where I grew up and studied Graphic Design. I also hold a Master in Cinematic Arts and an MA in Serial Storytelling from Germany. I am a filmmaker, an educator and a university professor. I have worked in the film industry for more than ten years. I could never identify myself or find a definitive answer for who I intrinsically am. I constantly find myself in a process of self-discovery through the things that I am doing. I like challenges, I always try to do things differently. I make films and tell stories. But I could never affirm that this defines who I am. I love motivating people and helping them create projects that they can bring to fruition. I could label myself a writer and an author but I prefer the term craftsman. I like to initiate projects regardless of whether they end up being completed, whether they fail or whether they only reach a handful of people - I get a real high from working and interacting with people and art, in all its various forms.

S: So, you do have a passion for helping others in their artistic projects?

M: Yes, definitely. This is probably the result of over ten years of exposure to the fascinating world of filmmaking. Working as a team generates a sense of collective power, a motivation to strive for a higher purpose; something which cannot be achieved through an average daily job.

S: When attempting to write books, where does your inspiration come from?

M: Most ideas are always brewing somewhere in my brain. The words are alive and they have tremendous power. Once they reach the threshold of being too annoying or painful, it's a cue for me to put them down on paper or out of my head. Very often, stories come as visual images. They are a combination of various concepts. Images, voices, observations. The next step is to ask myself the "What if" question. What if a person found themselves in a situation that required them to act in a certain way? Based on the previous observation, how would they then act or be-have? Two years ago, I remember being in Berlin with my wife and we were at the train station. We saw pigeons near the edge of the platform and I told her: Do you know that a pigeon whisperer's testimonial in court is not accepted? This is so because the pigeon whisperer is considered a thief or a liar because he steals other people's birds from the sky and claims them to be his. This idea has never left me. When I did my research, I found a true story about a Syrian refugee who had lost his pigeons because of the war. After he had become a refugee in Syria, he wanted to find home again by stealing the pigeons from the station.

S: When did you know that you wanted to become a writer?

M: From a very young age, I have always been fascinated by poetry and by people who are able to touch others with their words. I had a few attempts at writing poetry through expressing myself with words, but I never actually thought that I would be writing a book one day simply because it's not my domain of expertise. I have trained as a graphic designer, and I have worked in the film industry. Although I was writing short films at the time, writing was always something that came on the side. It was never something that I had consciously decided to do. It was just the result of all the other things I had attempted to do throughout my life.

S: As far as you can remember, what was the first thing that you wrote and when was it?

M: I think I was 18 years old at the time and I was reading a book by Nizar Qabbani. I was fascinated. What I can recall is that I was not happy with my life back then. As teenagers, many people struggle emotionally and they constantly try to belong. I went to my room and I started writing my first poem. Even when I was still at school, I would always find myself reading novels and stories and thoroughly enjoying my reading and comprehension classes. I remember reading David Copperfield by Charles Dickens and other novels that opened my mind to the amazing world of stories. When we started making short films with friends, we needed a script for our film in the making. Then came the desire to make another one. Writing started as a need. We needed someone who could write those scripts, so I did it. I have always felt a sense of joy at writing stories even just as a form of therapy.

S: In which environment does your writing thrive? How do you prepare yourself in order to be in the best mood?

M: I always like to immerse myself in certain kinds of music that have a specific inspiring rhythm, music that gives me a sense of isolation from my immediate surroundings. I need this to be able to feel totally immersed in the writing process. When I write stories, I don't type on the computer first; I write them in a notebook. The whole story is written down on paper because there is this quality of tangibility with the actual words; a beautiful connection between me and my writing; once I find myself immersed in that world, nothing can take me out of it. I feel at one with the words. Sometimes, I need to find a quiet place or space where I am not interrupted because I don't want to disrupt my thought patterns. I don't have any ritual. The most important thing for me is to plan the writing time and build it into a habit. I train myself daily to sit down and write my thoughts on paper. It's not always perfect. Things don't always work the way I want them to, but I have to keep doing it – until my brain gets used to it and the inspiration kicks in.

S: What happens when you experience the blank page syndrome?

M: I try to avoid it in the first place. I try to tell myself that it's not good to have a mental blank because it could go on for days or weeks. Even if I write one or two pages or 10 or 15 minutes a day, I feel satisfied and I know that I have accomplished my daily writing task. What really helps is to structure my stories ahead of time, way ahead of time, even before I start writing them. I actually try not to start putting words on paper unless I have a very solid structure. I need to know where the story is heading to, what are the chapters of the book, or how the characters will evolve from one point to the next.

S: What is your favourite genre of books?

M: I find it hard to identify genres or label books. Maybe I should, because it's important to know what kind of stories I intend to write. When I like a book, I read it because it has an interesting plot. I don't think about the genre prior to reading it. I even find it hard to label my own books under a certain genre. I do understand there are certain set of genres that help identify books, but who said these were the only genres? A book could have characteristics belonging to all genres, in just one story. I like to think of all fiction or stories in an abstract way; this allows me to avoid all labels of thinking. Categorising a work of art equals to setting limitations to it that were not present in the first place. This is not to say that genres don't exist, of course they do. The same applies for movies too. When I watch or make them, I just focus on the very essence of the story, the hero's journey and the dramatic arc.

S: Throughout your books, you have tackled the subject of spirituality. How did that come about and why did you develop an interest in spiritual stories?

M: Yes, this is a really good question. I don't know if I know the answer to this question. I think and I feel that this topic chose me, I didn't purposely choose it. If you think of spirituality as the change of the soul or a transition for a better understanding of the world and the inner self, then I think that all the characters in a book must undergo change. I feel that spirituality is about looking for the soul; it's about seeking to be a better person. Spirituality is about looking for love. It's always about change. It doesn't always have to be change for the best, but you can literally feel the changes within your own self. For example, when you watch any work of art and your senses enjoy it, this can be called a spiritual experience because not only have the characters experienced some form of change themselves, but you have, as well, whether you are a viewer or a reader. This beautiful quote about a Sufi mystic is very revealing: religion is being afraid to go to hell. Spirituality is about having been to hell but not wanting to go back. If you think about the personality of the characters, all characters; they have been wounded in a way, they have felt pain, they have morphed into being different people, trying to find their inner selves and trying to change through the pain they have experienced. This is why spiritual stories fascinate me because they touch on something very deep and very sentimental. And these feelings are universal in nature.

S: How long does it usually take to write a book?

M: It depends on the book. Some stories are harder than others because they require a lot more research and devising of plots. I would say maybe one year to two years from the moment I start writing the book. My stories tend to be shorter than average; they are novellas. Whenever I feel that the story arc has ended, this is where I stop. Maybe this is not an advantage, if we speak from the perspective of what sells the best on the market, but novellas are gradually getting a lot of appeal from readers and independent publishers as well. So, to answer your question, the focus on the depth of the story is my top priority; it does not matter how long the drafting of the book is going to take me.

S: Do you feel that being part of the diaspora or being away from home contributes to that feeling of spirituality and the need for the soul to find a home as well?

M: Definitely. You are always looking for home. The idea of not finding home is not just about losing the land or being away from your home country. I think we are all always continuously looking for home in our own different ways, in everything that we are doing. It's the place, it's the feeling that makes you recognise that comfort of the heart similar to the one you feel when you are at home.

S: But home could be an uncomfortable place as well, a place you want to escape from, right?

M: Definitely. I don't think there is a straightforward answer to this. Many people want to move out of their own homes and a lot of people who have lost their homes want to go back. I think the feeling of being away from home is a mirror for spirituality as well; the spirituality you are always seeking. It's a path, a long path along which you are always trying to find comfort and inner peace. I used to think (and I still do, to some extent) that losing your home was a curse. How could it not be? This loss has caused me to travel the world and I have met all sorts of people and experienced so many different places that I feel blessed to have seen. It has turned out to be a positive journey for me maybe because I have wanted to view it as such. For many others, (and I'm not saying I'm giving up on the idea of home) this is what they consider as the idea of loss but I have personally chosen to view it as hope because I had the urge to prove that, despite what had happened to me, something that was out of my control, I was going to be an optimist, a person who leaves a lasting impact in this world. It took many years of personal defeats and instances of helplessness before deciding to step up and face my own fears, my own desires and hopes of refinding a home. I think there could be a metaphor here or a piece of advice if you may call it: do not just look at what you don't have but always try to look beyond and above what you are capable of doing, achieving and giving. Do not limit yourself, do not set rigid boundaries. There are always ways to expand your horizons and do much more. Do you think your world is limited? It is not. The world is changing at a rapid pace. Its people are evolving and the concept of home is more than ever flexible. People want to mix with others who share different ideas, marry people from different cultures, try foreign foods, and experience the unknown. They are more aware of the idea of diversity. Again, this doesn't mean that I have given up on the idea of home or fighting for that cause with the best available means. Home could be anywhere; in friendship, in writing, and even in the simplest of things. I could find home in my own stories even though I have lost my original home. I would like to think that the entire world is my home.

S: What is the best advice you would give to beginner writers?

M: Believe in yourself and start writing. Write good stories that touch you first. Write stories that you want to tell and if you love what you do and if you are touched by your own writing and feel that it's coming from the heart, people will feel the same too. Don't wait for somebody to value your work. Do it first and good things will happen.

S: What would you tell young writers who are discouraged, who are scared of not writing good content or even not getting recognised after they take the steps towards success? Let's put it in this way: why should young writers still write today?

M: Because the world is hungry for good stories and it has always been. People want good stories. Do you realise how many stories in this world remain untold simply because someone out there is hesitant to take that major step forward? Stories are about changing people's lives, touching the reader from within, changing them at the very core of their being. A lot of research is now showing that kids who are not exposed to stories at an early age view the world completely differently from those who have been allowed to read and dream. For this is truly a special gift; the ability to see the world and understand the abstract and their inner world, even the outside world. When I was young, I remember watching The Lion King at the movies. This experience still resonates in my head and in my soul to this day. Something completely changed within me after watching it; the story, the music, the betrayal, the everything. One important characteristic differentiates us as human beings; the ability to understand the abstract. All other creatures do not possess this faculty. That's why we are different, we are unique in our own intrinsic way, and we have to utilise this tremendous blessing we have been gifted with. Stories are built around the abstract and about creating it and morphing it into something that could have an impact on the world.

S: I agree with you. Every story has a significance and we should not underestimate it. The content will reach people no matter the obstacles. People are hungry for good content. Once the story and good content is out there, it will find its way to people.

M: Right. In an interview with Nizar Qabbani, the Syrian poet, he said that the only thing that ends up dying is bad poetry or bad writing. Good art and good poems do not die, and they will always resonate with people even after thousands of years.

S: What do you do in your free time when you are not writing?

M: I'm always aware of time and the fact that time is always running away and slipping away from us. We have less time than the time we think we have. I am always trying to be conscious but not paranoid at the same time. I am constantly trying to take my projects to the next level. It's always a struggle to tame my hyperactive mind, but I try not to overexert myself. I just try my very best because there are stories that I love to tell people and that will have an impact on them everywhere.

S: What is your favourite book and author?

M: I think this question is similar to the genre question. I can't choose one book that I love over others. I read a lot of books and I love them all. There are many books that have touched me and ones that still do. The book that I enjoy the most is the book that stays with me; I carry it with me in my heart and I love it in a way that makes me want to read it again.

S: What are the most common mistakes that people make when writing?

M: It's that they write for themselves instead of writing for others. That's why, as a writer, you have to go back and understand the structure and the basics of story building and character transformation. You have to put your potential readers in your characters' shoes and have them identify with your characters. I think this is a common problem in many TV dramas as well; people do not invest enough time in building good characters and good plots. They have templates and they think these are always going to work. People and audiences are more aware of good stories when they see it and when they read it. Because they don't follow a good story arc, they end up writing diaries rather than writing appealing stories. That's a huge problem in the Arab world where people are not writing stories that inspire people, they write their own diaries or biographies but not stories with good characters and transformational arcs.

S: Exactly. You have a very good point here. My last question would be, what is the best piece of advice that you got, that you still remember, and the one you still go by?

M: If you want to write, please go ahead and write. I think nobody will ever teach you how to write, people can give you tips and everything else but you have to experience the personal process of trial and error many, many times, maybe even hundreds of times, until something works, until something holds together. There's a great book called "If you want to write" by Brenda Ueland and this could be one of my favourite non-fiction books. She talks about the importance of believing in yourself if you want to become a good writer. The author gives examples of Van Gogh and all those artists who really loved what they did and they just did it. They didn't care about people criticising them or not appreciating their art. They just went and did it. Yes, if you want to write just go ahead and do it.

S: What is your favourite sports?
M: I'm not so much a sports person. I enjoy exercising, specifically running. It gives me a sense of freedom and liberation and maybe even the feeling that I am flying. My mind is always racing with all these crazy thoughts. It has become a need for me to run weekly, if not daily, to just tame that overheating brain and that crazy monkey that's always dancing in my head. I try to run on a consistent, regular basis; I need that outlet to free my mind and my spirit. The much-needed peace.

S: Thank you for the conversation.
M: Thank you Sherouk for the interview. I really enjoyed it.
S: Me too.

Printed in Great Britain
by Amazon